Vanity Bagh

Anees Salim is an advertising professional employed with FCB-Ulka. His debut novel, *The Vicks Mango Tree*, was shortlisted for prestigious awards while his second novel, *Vanity Bagh*, won the Hindu Prize for Best Fiction 2013. His other published works include *Tales from a Vending Machine* and *The Blind Lady's Descendants*. He lives in Kochi with his wife and two children, Omar and Adah.

Praise for Vanity Bagh

'Rarely do you find a book by an Indian author that has style, substance and humour all in one delightful package.'

DNA

'The voice of the book, which is the best thing about it, preserves the timbre of detached narration.'

Hindu

'It's rare to come across a book in contemporary Indian English fiction that makes you giggle. Vanity Bagh does this, and that too while telling a gripping story of a terrorist.'

Firstpost

'It is a story that lulls you into thinking it is about the gentle ebb-and-flow of everyday normality, but is really a darkly funny and insightful look at the complexities of our lives.'

Deccan Herald

'Like an epic author he just looks at the events with a detached gaze that turns even tragedies and crises into just passing scenes from life's comic theatre.'

Frontline

Vanity Bagh

ANEES SALIM

PICADOR INDIA

First published in the Indian subcontinent 2013 by Picador India
an imprint of Pan Macmillan India, a division of
Macmillan Publishers India Limited
Pan Macmillan India,
707, Kailash Building 26, K.G. Marg, New Delhi – 110 001
www.panmacmillan.co.in

Pan Macmillan, The Smithson, 6 Briset Street, London EC1M 5NR,
Basingstoke and Oxford
Associated companies throughout the world
www.panmacmillan.com

ISBN 978-93-82616-41-2

This is a work of fiction. All characters, locations and events are fictitious. Any resemblance to actual events or locales or persons, living or dead, is entirely coincidental.

2

Typeset by Bembo Std 11.5/15.5 by Jojy Philip, Delhi 110 015
Printed and bound in India by Repro India Ltd

FSC www.fsc.org MIX Paper from responsible sources FSC® C047271

In memory of my father
M. Salim
(1927-2006)

I

I plead not guilty, Judge sahib. I bloody do.

~ Imran Jabbari (1985-   )

Long, long ago – about eighteen months ago, to be precise – my world shrank to the size of a mousetrap at the tap of a gavel on a very dark desk. It was a sunny day, so sunny that fair-skinned ladies decided to open their umbrellas, but the people crowding at the windows blocked the stream of light into the courtroom so completely that it might as well have been a rainy day.

There was a clock in the vicinity, out of sight. It let out the sound of a spoon hitting a metal plate every half hour, sending in premonitions of the long, empty years that would be handed to me by a judge who bore a close resemblance to a famous stand-up comedian.

The court split shortly after noon, people cleared from the windows, and there began the journey to the prison, which lasted a little under an hour, during the course of which I kept picturing my destination like I had done on my first trip to school.

It was a Friday and, just like on every Friday afternoon, there were long queues crawling into cinemas and big crowds pouring out of mosques – the two places I was going to miss ever so greatly.

At ten past two on the clock above the blue gates, the van reached its destination. From the outside, the prison looked like a school (the school, at first sight, had looked like a prison). There was a faint film of moss on the wall as if it were made of bronze and the rain had spread the first coat of patina over it. The gates opened with a dark enthusiasm, the van rolled morosely in.

Since that moment of driving through the tall gates I keep wondering if eighteen months have turned the outer wall a deep green, or if the prison authorities have had the inmates scrub it down to a light copper. In eighteen months I haven't had a chance to check on the outer wall; it might as well have been in outer space.

Exactly as in a school, there was a room where the shelves were crammed with ledgers and the walls hung with farewell pictures showing row after row of demure-faced men, the retiring ones highlighted with oversized garlands, the elaborate ends of which descended onto their laps and sat there like an origami garden sprouted from the crotch.

A warden in plain clothes sat by a window, the curtains of which were plaited like a girl's hair and secured with wooden rings, and wrote unhurriedly in a register as I told him the precise directions to a locality I might never see again.

'Vanity Bag?' he asked without looking up from the register.

'You mean "bag"?' He had never heard of our mohalla, maybe he had but didn't want to admit it, or he did not belong to the city.

'No, not "bag". Bagh.' I doodled the letters in the air as I uttered them, suddenly concerned about having wrong spellings on a page which would probably not be referred to for the next sixteen years. 'B-A-G-H. As in Mangobagh.'

'We have a spelling bee champion here?' The prison superintendent, a rather thin man with the face of a baboon, put his head round the half-door and looked unpleasantly at me. For a moment the wardens did not know whether to salute him or laugh. In the end, they decided to laugh. Clapping their hands, shaking their bellies, they laughed. I did not get the joke then, I still don't get it. Maybe there is not much of a joke; it could be a rule of the prison that wardens laugh at the superintendent's jokes even if they are sick jokes. They don't have the licence to kill you but they have the liberty to torture you with their weird sense of humour. Maybe that is how they compensate for their inability to get physical with you. They sure want to hit you once in a while, when they have had a bad day at work or a fight at home but, remembering the consequences in the nick of time, they pocket their clenched fists and go away. New government rules have made prisons a better place. You cannot beat up an inmate. Verbal abuse is out of the question. So is spitting on the face. No usage of mother-fucker, sister-fucker and brother-fucker (the last one is for gays). All those have now become a gross violation of human rights.

There is even a human rights officer who comes every month and sits under one of the gooseberry trees with a ledger open on his lap. If you have a grievance he is all ears. He will write down your complaint and make you sign under it, then sign it himself before passing it on to the concerned department. But people rarely tell him anything. When it is four on the double-faced clock above the blue gates, he brushes off the yellow leaves the tree has shed onto the complaint book and leaves the prison. Once two inmates marched up confidently to him as the wardens watched tensely; the braver of the two said the weekly meat curry was too watered down and tasted like something meant for cattle. But the officer firmly shook his head and dismissed the complaint as something that could not be treated as a human rights issue. The losers walked slowly back with fake smiles. The wardens smiled for real.

I wonder if the plain-clothes warden asks 'Bag?' every time he has a new inmate from our mohalla. Much to my nostalgic pleasure, I bump into people from Vanity Bagh every now and then, and the first thing I do is sniff. I sniff so hard that they think I have either caught a cold or, overcome with homesickness, I am struggling to keep my nose from running. But in reality I am just trying to be a dog, to take in the smell of the mohalla, of its alleys and backyards, food stalls and florists, guile and innocence, innumerable drains and the lone attar shop that sits next to Suleiman's Homeopathic Clinic. Sniffing yields nothing, though, for once you have slipped into the prison uniform everyone smells pretty much the same. Everyone smells of despair and, sometimes, bleaching powder.

Last summer a stubby little man with restless eyes and busy fingers came over from D-Block to meet me. He said we used to be near neighbours in the other world; his family lived directly above the Bata outlet, though I didn't remember spotting him near the Bata store or anywhere else in Vanity Bagh. He wanted tips from me, tips on surviving the three months that had been slapped on him. He was typical Sub Jail material: small crime, brief term. He had been charged with the kind of swindling most kids do in their schooldays, but the poor chap did it with a big company that has half an English name, a proper logo and trademark, and ended up here because the Sub Jail was running beyond capacity. I told him there were no particular tips to surviving a prison. Just be yourself. That is the trick. And he said that was exactly what his boss wanted everyone in the office to do. Just be yourself. And that was what he had done with the office money. Leaning against a pillar, we laughed until we remembered we were convicts.

I asked him about Vanity Bagh the way people ask after old friends, and he talked about it as if it were a friend-turned-foe. He didn't care much about it and, still worse, he would be moving his family to another neighbourhood once his three-month term expired. I asked how the mohalla was doing. He shrugged. I asked after the well-known people and the popular establishments of the area. He shrugged again. It was as if he had made up his mind to shrug the mohalla off his back.

The three months went like two weeks; when he came to the garden one afternoon to say a quick goodbye I shook his hand longer than a handshake normally lasts. The longer the handshake, I thought, the deeper I would rub my fingerprints onto his. And no matter how brief his stopover would be, he was certain to leave my fingerprints unknowingly on several things in the mohalla: trees, lampposts, walls, doors, ATMs, railings.

It was one of those months when people were released in large numbers. Some left after elaborate goodbyes that made you painfully jealous of their freedom; others vanished as quietly as in a jailbreak, their absence noticed later by the vacant seats in the TV Room and the workplaces that needed new hands.

The Carpentry Room was suddenly short of three men, the Handicraft Room four, Kitchen seven, but it was the Book Room that was worst hit. It had sent thirteen bookmakers out to the free world. One morning we were getting a patch of land behind the water tanks ready for growing spinach when a head warden strolled up with a clipboard and pencil. His shadow paced the freshly raked earth, fat and funny. At regular intervals he pointed the pencil at an inmate and said 'You', and the chosen one stared solemnly down as if he had been picked by a firing squad. Once used to roaming free among the ancient trees, soaking up the sun and occasionally slipping behind a tree to smoke a contraband cigarette, once used to all this luxury, nobody wanted an indoors job. The outdoors fill you with sounds and sights, a long list of them: the best sound is that of trucks, as small in your mind's eye as toys, tearing down the distant expressway; the best sight from a prison is a silent aeroplane disappearing into an Everest of clouds. It makes you want to get out of prison one day and do well in life. The most disturbing sight always awaits me beneath the loose stones near the bamboo clumps. I lift them occasionally in the course of weeding the garden steps, and an acute sadness creeps up on me at the sight of snails lurking under the lichened stones. They are reminders of the slow years I have to live through. Apart from that, I have no issues with the outdoors.

Even the sun doesn't like to linger around a prison interior for long, where sometimes it is hard to tell solid things from shadows. It beats me as to why there are still people who would give anything to land an indoors job; when you are destined to live in a prison, why would you want to spend your days in another prison inside it?

I was grateful that I was not deemed fit for one of the rooms. Not yet.

'You,' the head warden said exactly a minute after I had heaved a sigh of relief at being spared. I didn't look up from the shallow pit I was digging with a stick.

'You, 111,' he said again, rubbing the sole of his boot against the gravel. 'I am putting you in the Book Room.'

That sounded like news of the death of someone who owed you a lot of money.

'Come join this group,' he said, pointing his pencil at three old men, all of whom were big book haters, to judge from the heavy frowns on their faces. I equally hated books. But in a prison you can't pick and choose a career.

The Book Room is the quietest of all workplaces in the Central Prison. It is many blocks from the nearest sign of human inhabitation. The silence that surrounds it makes you think of a library. It even looks like a library, for that matter, with same-size books, darkly stained shelves and ceiling fans suspended from long poles. But the books here have only blank pages, which makes it a library of unwritten books and unforced silence. The blade of a paper-cutting machine occasionally swishes through the uneven edges of freshly made books and makes a light thud.

Books are born in near silence. No wonder libraries are such quiet places. Edges trimmed, they are passed onto my table. I bind them. At twenty-four, that is my calling.

Even my ammi, who had sat in the third row of the packed courtroom with her lower lip pushed out in anticipation of bad news, would not have imagined me ending up among books eighteen months after my fate had been officially sealed. She had been praying silently through the morning of the verdict, a tasbih moving through her fingers like a brown baby snake. The beads froze between her fingers when the judge cleared his throat and opened his mouth to pronounce the verdict.

> Imran Jabbari has been found guilty of all the charges
> and is sentenced to sixteen years of imprisonment.
> – Justice P. R. Nariman (-2012)

The tasbih tumbled onto the court floor without so much as a tiny tinkle. Ammi followed suit, shrieking.

II

11/11 is Mangobagh's private little 9/11.
~ *City Chronicle* (1959-   )

The first days in the Book Room were the hardest, and the bleakest. Every place I had forcibly turned into a comfort zone appeared to have been condemned overnight and knocked down without an eviction notice. I missed the vegetable patch we had been working on, and the shade under the bamboos, where the grass was greener and park-like. I craved the sun, cigarettes and the right frame of mind to play that solo mental game in which I jumped the jail when everyone was lost in thoughts about the other world or merely looking the other way.

The Book Room, a long hall with a blue door set at either end, had a depressing smell of, what else, books. More depressing if you had hated books in the other life; in my life before the prison, I had been allergic to books, even to newspapers and magazines. So I was as big a misfit in the Book Room as a temple would have been in our mohalla. I found myself looking forward to someone getting tired of my clumsiness and reporting me to the superintendent: Inmate No. 111 has no knack for bookmaking nor any interest. Gardening is his vocation. Transfer him to the greens. Let him grow vegetables.

Then one day, one Friday afternoon, the miracle happened.

Miracles happen on Fridays. On Fridays alone.
– The madwoman outside the masjid (-2007)

Happening without omens, it lasted less than a minute. I had just finished binding a book and was sizing up my lack of talent for the job when it happened. It all began with an impulse and ended with a revelation: something is seriously wrong with me or the world.

I had casually opened the book and glanced inside, expecting to see nothing. There was, of course, nothing on the page I had opened the book to, but my eye caught something grey and grainy underneath, like bits of lead stuck between the pages. I turned the leaf but found nothing on the new page either, except the promise of something grainy and grey on the page below. If one impulse had led me to open the book another insisted I stay on the page and stare at it, until I saw an alphabet, then a word, a sentence, a paragraph, a page, a story. This could be another game my mind played, like the game of a daylight jailbreak, where I get three lives as in computer games and the guards get bonus points if they shoot me between the eyes. I closed the book, and opened it after a while. Blank pages. But if I stared long enough I knew the words would be right back, ready to tell a story. My story.

Every third Saturday, a makeshift tent is erected near the front garden and four doctors sit behind different tables set outside hearing distance of each other, as if one is not sure of his diagnosis and doesn't want the other to overhear. Three of them are armed with stethoscopes; the one without a stethoscope, whom I first took for a priest minus the cassock, is a psychiatrist and to the best of my knowledge he is the only psychiatrist in the world who has decided against sporting a French beard. If you have a mental issue come talk to me, his smile seems to say. Inmates frequently go to him and complain about sleeplessness or hypertension, hoping to get some sleeping pills or even a recommendation for parole. All they get is counselling, though. In the week after I first spotted words appear on blank pages as on a magic slate, I considered consulting him and getting myself counselled, consoled and cured. Then I thought: why? What harm can it cause me? Maybe this is a rare skill, like mirror writing, which one in a million is blessed with. Maybe God has sent me this facility because He willed me to read my own story as if I haven't lived it myself.

The next time I opened a book, a ray of sunlight angled in through a cracked roof tile and fell on a page, illuminating no words. There were, in fact, thousands of words, maybe more, only that the naked eye couldn't see them straightaway.

Every night thousands of stars appear in the sky.
Blame it on your eyes if you see only a few.
– Professor Suleiman Ilahi (1949-)

I scrunched up my eyes for a couple of minutes and there appeared words, and words formed people, people formed places. The first place this nearly invisible opening chapter sketched was Vanity Bagh. That meant the chapters in this book were in perfect order.

Barely a mile long, Vanity Bagh is a long queue of old buildings waiting at the Char Bazaar intersection for the light to change so that they can trot down the zebra crossing and join the architectural revolution that has been sweeping across Mangobagh since the turn of the millennium. But the green light never comes on for them, and they remain standing on either side of a reasonably wide and unreasonably busy road. That is one thing I have always noticed about Vanity Bagh. It is always busy, unreasonably so because it houses no important places – no government office where you get important licences or certificates for a bribe, no famous shop which runs discount sales all year round, no eminent fakir who can cure even Hepatitis B by merely blowing into your ears, nothing of the crowd-pulling sort. All it has is a row of dusty green colonnaded structures with balconies made of wood and the railings of wrought iron. All the buildings are treated with the same measure of negligence, and not a single one of them has seen a lick of paint since Bushra Jabbari, my Ammi, set foot in the mohalla as a young bride.

> In my memory these buildings haven't
> changed a bit in thirty years.
> – Bushra Jabbari (1962-)

Amidst this horrid stretch of masonry stands Masjid-e-

Mosavi, a tiny, green-domed mosque where the whole neighbourhood comes to pray on Fridays. Next to its arched entrance is a narrow external stairway that leads to the terrace from which pigeons fly out five times a day at the sound of the azan.

> Don't sit on the steps. And don't smoke here.
> This is a place of worship. No place for idlers.
> – Kareem Jabbari (1953-)

Though we were not highway robbers or rippers or something even half-acclaimed as Abu Hathim sahib, the mohalla always thought there was something utterly fishy about our gang. The mohalla-wallahs knew where to bump into us, and they tried their best not to. We hung around Mogul Bakery, which produces probably the best kebabs in the whole of Mangobagh, or sat on the wall that had been built by the Railways to stop encroachments into their territory. When a police patrol crept through the mohalla we vanished into the alley near the Irani Café, where we lounged in the shade of Abu Hathim sahib's two-storeyed house, ducking when he walked up to an upstairs window to spray paan juice into the alley.

We called ourselves '5½ Men', though there were a whole six of us. But everything in the mohalla has a strange name, and a strange story. The imam of the Masjid-e-Mosavi once said our area had been named after the wife of the British engineer who built the bridge across the Moosa River a century ago. But did a lady named Vanity ever exist on planet earth? I seriously doubt the authenticity of this story, even though the imam in question happens to be my own father.

The mohalla-wallahs are so obsessed with spinning yarns and naming things that they haven't even spared a tree that stands bang opposite the mosque. They call it Franklin, as if it were born to Christian parents and even goes to St Thomas Basilica on Sundays along with the Pintos who run a garage a few blocks from the tree. In spite of its appearance, which borders on an antique variety of grandeur, the tree has not much significance in the history of the street. To be more precise, it is nothing but a criminal waste of nature's time. Franklin bears neither flowers nor fruit, and starts shedding leaves only in late autumn, sprouting new ones when spring is almost out of sight; by the time its branches sport the first load of tender leaves other trees along the street will already have pupae under their foliage.

The only person who had any memory of the tree as a sapling died a couple of years ago at the age of 105. He, as a small boy, had witnessed Father Franklin plant it in the sepia-coloured mud of Vanity Bagh nearly a century ago.

Pather Praklin frayed and frayed and
balked and balked around the free.
– Ghulam Chacha (1902-2007)

In Ghulam Chacha's ragged memory, Father Franklin eternally circled the sapling, spraying holy water on its leaves before launching himself on a preaching trip through Mangobagh. For the first few years, the sapling stood sulking across the street from the mosque, nameless, guarded from the preying tongues of cattle with a tubular fence made of mesh. Then somebody, probably Ghulam Chacha, gave it the name of the priest who was nutty enough to walk around a little sapling while reading from the Bible.

The day the *City Chronicle* renewed the legend of Franklin in its Sunday edition – sometimes these newspapers have so much free space they write about any crap, even about garbage disposal and eunuchs – we started hating the tree. What was a tree that reeked of Christianity doing in a Muslim neighbourhood? People started talking about felling it; they were furious that it had been planted by a Christian who must have bribed a few dozen Muslims into kafirs. Probably the Pintos had been practising Muslims a century ago; the mohalla-wallahs were almost sure that Moses, the senior-most member of the Pinto clan, had been called Moosa before his conversion. His wife was still called Fatima, whom the mohalla-wallahs now suspected of secretly fasting during Ramzan.

> I saw Fatima Auntie buying dates from
> Mogul Bakery during last Ramzan. Also haleem.
>
> – Aasia Jamal (1992-)

No one normally believed Aasia Jamal: she once said she had won, through a draw of lots as part of an advertising campaign, the chance to dine with Irfan Pathan, but declined to go as cricket didn't interest her much. She said no to Irfan? Yusuf would have been an easier-to-believe lie. But this time around, Aasia Jamal seemed to be speaking the truth. The Pintos were suddenly frowned upon and discussed as the sort of people who would trade anything for money, even the religion they were born into.

Leave the Pintos alone, the imam said. And let Franklin be.

The Pintos were left alone; all of a sudden the mohalla-wallahs could not care less about Franklin, except for Jinnah, who was the devoutest Muslim among us. He said he would drive mercury-coated nails into the tree. He even produced a handful of nails as proof of his indignation, but he had no clue where to find mercury. 'But I'll somehow finish this fucking tree,' he said. But something, probably a quick mental picture of the street without its trademark tree, deterred him from working out a new plan for vengeance. One day he whipped out his penknife with a flourish, as if he were going to fell Franklin with it, and started carving the name of our gang on its rock-like skin, working dedicatedly a whole afternoon until the bark blunted the blade. Then he used a screwdriver. But the older name appeared to have been etched deeper into the mind of the mohalla, and the tree continued to be known by its Christian name. '5½ Men', engraved like a declaration of calf love, remained only physically, catching the eye of people as they stared out of vehicles bumping through the choked street. They probably didn't even wonder what that odd number stood for. As a gang we aspired to be nothing less than a nightmare, dreaded for a whole set of beastly qualities, but all we naturally had was a turtle's instinct to shrink up and stay in our shell at the faint wail of a police siren.

We dreamed the dream of the poor – to be rich and, circumstances permitting, famous – and we had an unlikely role model, who didn't come from film posters or sports pages but lived right amidst us, in the alley beside the Irani

Café, in a rambling, well-guarded building that was Abu Hathim sahib's home and refuge rolled into one. By the time we were tall enough to reach up to his waist, he had ceased to be a hero for most of the mohalla-wallahs. He had lost a leg, and the ability to make people salaam with great humility. But childhood heroes die a slow death, and Abu Hathim sahib continued to live in our memories as the man who had drafted Mangobagh's riot charts, who had settled feuds between gangsters, guarded nightclubs in Begum Bazaar and Broadway and, most of all, stood in the middle of the street with his hands behind his back and chest puffed up as bulldozers rolled in to knock down a new illegal housing colony. In our mind's eye, the legend of Abu Hathim still strode on two sturdy legs, though we could clearly hear the thump of his crutches as he picked his way to the windows to spray the alley with paan juice.

Zulfikar, who had the temerity to claim Abu Hathim sahib as his Ammi's first cousin, looked up from the splatter of paan juice on the alley stones one evening and snapped his fingers for attention. 'Can't we be somebody like Abu Hathim sahib?'

The stains on the stones looked so much like blood that I wondered if Abu Hathim sahib had become terminally ill.

'One-legged like him?' asked Jinnah, laughing.

'I mean, can't we form a gang?' Zulfikar said. 'Like he did when he was our age?'

Abu Hathim sahib had made his mark very early in life, having been booked for murder at the age of nineteen, acquitted several times before he reached twenty and ranked as one of the top terrors of Mangobagh when he was hardly twenty-one. And look at us – we were already twenty-two or more, and nonentities.

'Can't we?' Zulfikar asked.

The idea touched me like a cold, invisible thing, like the hand of a ghost, and I remember shivering slightly. Maybe a cold wind blew through the mohalla when I first heard about it but, looking back, I want to believe that it was a foreboding that touched me like a hand – a firm, clammy hand. When the momentary chill passed, I could see beyond the end of the alley, I could see the future and our place in it.

'Can't we?' Zulfikar asked again.

If the six of us could roll ourselves into one big Abu Hathim sahib, we could probably rule the mohalla, we could even recreate history in a small way. As on a huge video wall I could see the gang doing many things, the same things Abu Hathim sahib had probably done when we had been children: guarding the mohalla, being salaamed by the mohalla-wallahs; collecting hafta, being salaamed by the mohalla-wallahs; making a fortune, being salaamed more by the mohalla-wallahs; beating up the mohalla-wallahs, being salaamed still more by them; and finally losing a leg.

The year was 2007 and the season late summer, when twilight came early and made Vanity Bagh look like the gloomiest place on earth. As darkness spread in the alley we heard Abu Hathim sahib cough and clear his throat, followed by the thumps his crutches made on the floor. A fresh shower of paan juice landed on the alley floor, and I found myself wondering again if Abu Hathim sahib was living out his last days. When the thuds of the crutches, as precise as clockwork, faded away, Zulfikar said it was time someone stepped into the shoes that had been lying vacant since Abu Hathim sahib had his right leg amputated. 'If we don't, someone else will,' he said.

Police are in the mohalla, looking for two young men who beat up the Bata manager.
– Passer-by (-)

Jinnah and Zia looked at each other, almost lovingly, then walked hurriedly towards the end of the alley where there was the railway line, beyond which, hidden behind big trees and draped with dusty vines, stood a dilapidated flint structure.

The next afternoon we met on the stairway that stood next to the mosque like a wooden ladder left leaning against the building, and sat listening to Zulfikar as pigeons landed on and took off from the terrace with an angry flutter of their wings. What had sounded like a life-changing idea in a nutshell now turned out to be something grossly self-centred as he added one detail after another to his brainwave. When he said 'gang', Zulfikar meant *his* gang. Maybe he had spent the whole week imagining himself seated on the throne Abu Hathim sahib had vacated soon after a crude bomb had been hurled at him just outside Mogul Bakery; Zulfikar must have pictured the five of us standing behind his chair wearing dark goggles, hands cupped over our crotches like soccer players.

'The best idea you have ever had, Zulfikar,' Zia said, his small eyes wide open in mock wonder. We all faked admiration for our new chief, and Zulfikar was on the verge of self-coronation when we erupted into a round of synchronized laughter, which slowly grew in volume and emptiness until

Zulfikar got up and climbed down the stairway. He disappeared from our sight just after Franklin, his black T-shirt blending into the darkness behind the row of public lavatories. The laughter brought the imam to the window, where he stood with his hands on the ledge and glared at me, just at me as if he didn't see the rest of the gang, and they fell quiet, more out of respect for me than for him.

You can laugh at a brilliant idea, but you can't laugh it off altogether. Knowing this, Zulfikar came back the next evening with amendments to his idea and a big smile. The imam had closed the green, slatted windows soon after he finished the evening azan in a style that made the mohalla-wallahs wonder whether to laugh or complain to the Muslim Welfare Board. But he had not turned the louvres down; light from the prayer hall sieved through the slats and fell on the damp steps, glinting on the moss like dew.

'I don't want to be the leader,' Zulfikar said with the air of someone who was making a sacrifice for mankind, 'if you people don't like it.'

'We people certainly don't like it,' said Jinnah. He was the bluntest of the six, looks-wise and otherwise. 'And nobody can be my leader.'

'Yes, that was what I was about to tell you too,' Zulfikar said. 'Nobody is going to be anybody's leader. It's a gang without a leader.'

(Jinnah, who had been brainwashed by his Ammi into joining Dey's Mart the next week as a shop assistant, changed his mind. Who wants to fake smiles at customers when you could stare shop owners into paying the weekly hafta?)

So the gang would have no leader, though time and again

Zulfikar would try to strike the pose of one with a simple matchstick, which he placed in a corner of his mouth and pushed around with the tip of his tongue, an act that made him look like he was sneering at the listlessness of our mohalla and the oddity of its name.

Since the gang was headless it couldn't afford to be nameless. Long hours were spent on the steps, smoking and arguing, trying to sell one's own choice, not willing to buy what others thought the most fitting name for the gang. When the debate got too loud the imam opened the window and glared out, not seeing anyone, but staring at a particular spot which he imagined to be the head of his own son. He tugged at his long, hennaed beard frequently, conveying to the vague outlines on the stairs that he was enraged to the point of dialling 101.

'Don't sit on the stairs,' he yelled out. 'And don't smoke here.'

We quickly wrapped our fingers around the cigarettes, hiding their glowing tips in our palms, and the imam stomped off to the far side of the prayer hall, only to reappear at the window at regular intervals. After the window had been thrown open and slammed shut the third time that night, Jinnah made an observation. 'I think the imam sahib hennas his pubic hair too.'

There was a long moment of silence in the stairwell.

'I'm sorry, Imran,' Jinnah said after a while. 'I didn't mean to make fun of your Abba.'

'It's all right,' I forced a laugh, swallowing hard.

What remained of the evening was spent in hushed parleys, and the session was finally cut short by a drizzle, which made us look up in surprise, as if we expected Abu Hathim sahib to stand on the rooftop, squirting betel juice down on us through the V of his fingers placed against his lips.

We found a name for the gang the next evening as we sat under Franklin, watching the slow traffic on the main road. But it would be another month or so before Mangobagh would find us out, and offer us opportunities, possibilities and a story we would want the children of Vanity Bagh to grow up listening to.

III

If this city had a WTC,
they would have bombed it as well.
~ Public Prosecutor (-)

On my way from the Food Hall to the Book Room I found it under one of the gooseberry trees. It lay on the cobbled path, face down, waiting to be trampled. The moment I picked it up I understood the real meaning of feather-light. It means lighter than air and ready to float away. The feather was a fluffy yellow, fairly big; it must have slipped off the plume of a pale yellow, innocent-looking bird as it flew over the prison. I have no clue which bird; I don't even wonder which bird. Birds don't interest me; rules do.

Rule No. 7 (a varnished board outside the superintendent's office lists out sixteen of them in white enamel) says inmates are not supposed to collect things. And, as if in a reaffirmation of Rule No. 7, our uniforms are completely bereft of pockets. The wardens' uniforms have plenty of them; it's an open declaration that they collect things, mostly money. The last time Ammi was here she bribed the sentry even if there was absolutely no need to: it was Visitors' Day when purses usually remain shut and doors open. The sentry did not even mention a bribe in the usual roundabout way sentries do. She must have gone up to him and volunteered, 'Please take this money. I have brought it for you all the way from Vanity Bagh.' She has a talent for corrupting even the most honest warden in service.

None of the rules enamelled on the board say an inmate should exercise restraint on following his impulses. So I quickly went down to my knees and whisked off the feather from the floor before boots or bare feet could trample it. It was as light as yourself in that recurring dream in which a beautiful, convent-educated girl insists you marry her (and in each version the dream bursts like a bubble just before you could comply).

Noticing me crouching on the cobbled path, a warden raised his voice from the veranda, 'Are you planning to pee there, son?' Inside the prison walls, 'son' is the abbreviation of 'son of a whore' or worse.

I sprang to my feet and continued to the Book Room, the feather secreted on my person. Though I trod carefully across the courtyard, like a woman whose movements are controlled by the fear of a miscarriage, I was somehow convinced that the feather had already been damaged. But it miraculously survived the trip – the tip was a bit crushed, that's all.

Why did I take the trouble of smuggling in something even a bird had considered good riddance? Only when I stood behind the worktable piled with stacks of paper did I find an answer. To give my books of magical pages more legitimacy,

I had unknowingly been craving a bookmark. When you are in captivity, every act, no matter how unreal it is, needs all possible accessories to create an air of make-believe.

There were five freshly bound books on the table, the fruit of my half a day's labour. I opened the one on top, half-expecting to hear the squeal of hinges as if I were opening the door of a library. I placed the feather between the pages – blank pages, of course – and closed the book. The tip of the feather stuck ungracefully out of the book as if a little bird had landed on the book I was reading and I had snapped it shut in a fit of rage, trapping the poor thing inside. But it looked a decent bookmark notwithstanding. To retrieve the feather and keep it in the tool box with rolls of twine and a little bunch of needles, I opened the book. And there you were – the miracle had happened again: in the few minutes I had kept the book closed its pages had been filled with words.

'Work, son, work,' a warden called out to me from the other end of the aisle as he did every afternoon after lunch. He would then pace down to the tower of books on the far side of the room and back to the barred door two times over, just to ease his post-lunch heartburn. After the routine walk, he would undo the top two buttons of his shirt and collapse onto a chair; his siesta lasted exactly twenty-five minutes. It is the time of the day when every official, with the exception of the sentries, sinks deeper into his chair and closes his eyes for just a minute; he is shaken awake half an hour or so later by the renewed call of duty. I have fixed this hour for jumping the jail. The date I haven't made up my mind about yet.

Once the warden had settled into his chair and started to snore – almost immediately – I opened the book at the page that now had the luxury of a bookmark. Words, words and all of them about the life I had lived until they handcuffed me and brought me here in a rattling van on a grey Friday.

I read those words, fascinated.

If I wrote down the names of our gang-members one below the other on a sheet of paper, the oddity would have struck you instantly. You should see them together to understand the absurdity of this coincidence. We ourselves never noticed it in the first place and eventually it was Zia, who had this bad habit of digging deep into things and coming up with laughable trivia of life, who said we all had the names of Pakistani politicians. We could not stop laughing for a whole afternoon.

In our mohalla it's quite normal, you can even call it inevitable, to be named after someone rich and famous from Pakistan. But everyone in the area doesn't have politicians' names like our gang-members do. Some have the names of singers, some of actors, some others of cricketers. I, for instance, am named after Imran the cricketer, and not Imran the politician. (The mohalla-wallahs always name their children after people with successful professions. It was Imran's own fault that he joined politics and lost his wife and everything nice to more successful people.)

Though the imam was a big fan of cricket, he had no knowledge of the rules and tactics involved; he didn't know what a night watchman was supposed to do, nor could he tell Dicky Bird from Billy Bowden. Like people with marginal knowledge of cricket, he attributed the fall of each and every wicket to perfect aim alone, and occasionally poked fun at

Ashish Nehra for handling the ball more awkwardly than the girls in the mohalla handled catapults. He named my younger brother Wasim – he, incidentally, is a lefty.

The street had a Benazir too. She was the youngest daughter of Mir sahib, the chubby little man who owned Mogul Bakery and a string of less successful enterprises across the city, who was the richest guy in Vanity Bagh if you counted white money alone. If black money and encroached properties were allowed to be counted, nobody in the area could beat Abu Hathim sahib in wealth and in wile. Even kids in the area would vouch for that.

I had a short fling with Mir sahib's last-born. Imran and Benazir! Doesn't it remind you of the stories that surfaced shortly after a human bomb killed Benazir? Imran and Benazir! Benazir and Imran! The mohalla-wallahs have no qualms when it comes to gossiping even about the dead and the retired. They know bitching about the deceased and the fallen is not a nice thing to do, but they don't believe in doing just nice things alone. The Benazir from our mohalla was very nearly sexy. I gave her eight out of ten. Our gang-members grudged her just five on the night we were grading the girls in the mohalla – girls from our own families didn't get any grade, they simply did not exist in this rushed census. Benazir was tall, even without her high heels – with which I was equally in love – she was almost my height. Her curls were very curly and always stuck out of the shawl she wore over her head, which gave her the permanent air of a refugee fleeing from the Afghan border. What spoiled her looks were her lips, each the size of my thumb, which she kept painted in light pink or shocking copper. In Jinnah's opinion, hers were the kind of lips that looked good only in a blue film.

They lived directly above the bakery, and her windows, doing utmost justice to the name of the family establishment, were in Mogul style and overlooked the street. During the first season of our romance I used to hang around the bakery even after the other guys had gone home, feeling a pang of anxiety when passing buses and overburdened trucks blocked my view of her room. I feared her windows would be erased from the masonry by the time the building came back to view. The things people think up in love! But the windows were always there, and she would be behind one of them as long as I was on the street, combing her hair. Sometimes I stayed out so late that I saw bats returning to Franklin after their long haul over the city. I never went home of my own accord; sometimes the imam sent Wasim out in search of me, at other times Mir sahib came out of the building for a smoke and stood on the sidewalk, looking lovingly at the building, as if he were serenading his own home.

Her wedding was the grandest affair Vanity Bagh had witnessed since her elder brother's. Even Abu Hathim sahib, who rarely came out of his home after a crude bomb had driven him indoors, came to bless the couple, surrounded by a band of frowning men whose bulging pockets outlined the shape of country-made pistols. Why Abu Hathim sahib? Even I went, and made a discovery: contrary to what is widely believed and poetically expressed in couplets, there is no lump hardening in your throat as you watch your ex marry. The feast was on the rooftop, under a canopy of red-and-ochre concentric designs, and I helped myself liberally to the lamb biryani a famed cook from Hyderabad had been roped in for. I even freaked out with Jinnah and Zia, who wanted to swap their frayed footwear with the district collector's expensive leather shoes when the stairs were deserted. They took turns to slip their feet into the black, spotless pair like in the 'Cinderella' story. Jinnah's feet were a size ten while Zia and the collector had smaller, daintier feet. And that settled it. Crouching on the steps, Zia tied the shoelaces as slowly as if the shoes were his own and went home whistling, leaving behind his rubber slippers with Hulk Hogan's face on the insole for the collector. The bride's father was hugely embarrassed and apologetic, offering to get a replacement from Dey's Mart, but the collector laughed the offer off and, singing praises of the Hyderabadi biryani, leaped over the puddles to his car. For the rest of the night, Mir sahib hired Jinnah to keep an eye on the guests' footwear. We ranked it as the top joke of 2006.

So Benazir did not marry Imran; she married a paunchy television dealer called Shooja and left the mohalla, promptly returning every year to labour in Bismi Maternity Centre.

The street even had a man named Pervez, a tiny creature primly dressed in clothes that were in vogue when Amitabh Bachchan was the official angry young man of the nation. It was hard to spot him without a smile on his close-shaven baby face. He was always at the bus shelter, awaiting a bus that never came. A tattered copy of *Good Housekeeping* tucked under an arm, an imitation leather attaché case dangling from a hand, he would stare pensively past the intersection and pick pockets with long, nifty fingers. I had once seen him at work, and what a smooth operator he was. Once a pocket had been picked, which he did with lightning speed, he would carefully place the attaché case on the floor and pore over *Good Housekeeping* until his victim boarded a bus and was gone. Then he would disappear into a neighbouring alley, probably to stow away the loot, and resurface in a short while, all smiles as ever. He was a nice little gentleman living quietly out of commuters until he went into bad company, joining a gang of young drug peddlers from another area who rode their remodelled motorbikes through Vanity Bagh like snowmobiles, swaying through traffic as the wind played in their long hair. They were all picked up from a mall the day Mangobagh's narcotic cell had a new, ruthless chief, and we heard nothing more of Pervez and his new friends.

Our own gang found its name one early evening during the listless monsoon of 2007, precisely a day after Jinnah had made a reference to the imam's pubic hair while we had been sitting on the stairway. The name, like the very idea of the gang, came from Zulfikar.

5 ½ Men.

– Zulfikar Faizudin (1984–?)

No one spoke for a while; you simply didn't want to say something to an odd name like that and be mocked for your judgement for the rest of your life. As in every situation that leaves you indecisive, each waited for the first response to come from somebody else.

'Anyone in disagreement, please raise your hand,' Zulfikar said.

Zia readily held up a hand.

'You don't like the name?' Zulfikar asked calmly. 'Reason?'

'I like the name very much. That's why I raised my hand.'

No one even cared to laugh at Zia. We were too busy deciding if the name was awesome or awful, because we didn't know any adjective that existed in between.

'All for it then?' Zulfikar asked, a matchstick quivering in a corner of his mouth. 'Can we freeze on it?'

There was a voice of dissent, though, which ironically came from a person who had never spoken a proper word in his whole life. Yahya, another one of us with a popular Pakistani name, as you can see, was born dumb. But he was not dumb dumb, he was smart dumb. When the Almighty pressed the mute button on him at the assembly line, He gave Yahya something exceptional in damages, and rolled him out into the noisy world with a set of remarkably big ears that heard things no one else did: ants marching across asbestos roofs, beetles sneezing, goats imitating radio jingles, rain-clouds preparing to dissolve into a shower over the city and even the squeal of the public lavatory door as the ghost of Iskander, a young man who died from having too much fake cocaine, went in to pee.

Yahya read lips as well, and he read them more fluently than we read the Quran. And on that day of christening our gang his eyes never left Zulfikar's nicotine-stained lips as the latter explained how he had arrived at that peculiarly odd name. It was a simple trick, Zulfikar said: he had counted Yahya only as half a member because of his handicap. I secretly thought he should be whipped for saying that in Yahya's presence.

When you make fun of someone's handicap,
Allah reserves a bigger one for you.
– The madwoman outside the masjid (-2007)

Yahya mimed his resignation from the gang, tearing up an imaginary contract and throwing it into a bin that did not even exist (during that furious act of cutting up an indenture and throwing it to the wind, only the wind was real and pretty gusty). He kicked the wall, slapped Franklin, spat. But when no one paid any attention he stopped behaving like that and sat down on the stone bench, staring at a bottle crown partly buried in mud. His fingers, which were his lips, would not part and utter a word for the rest of the evening.

'All of us will have our wrists tattooed "5½ Men",' Zulfikar proclaimed. 'Agreed?'

Yahya sprang to his feet and, swinging his hands almost comically, tore down the street. For the next two days there was no sign of him. He was the kind of person who was easily and greatly missed. I strolled down the smelly lane where he lived in a lopsided house that looked like a coop built for ostriches, whistling a radio-station anthem which was our code. He didn't whistle back, though I knew he was watching me from behind a curtain. But on the third evening, just when Zulfikar was tinkering with the idea of renaming the gang, Yahya was back under Franklin, laughing and thumping us on the back, his fingers talkative once again, his wrist ready to be tattooed.

Going home with a tattooed wrist equalled doing a striptease in front of the imam. So I asked the tattoo-wallah to do it on my upper arm instead of the wrist, and in a much smaller version than what was already on Zulfikar's wrist. And, believe me, mine looked the best of the six. Or of five-and-a-half, as Zulfikar would have put it.

IV

When the city was burning,
Imran Jabbari, a devoted son,
was attending to his very sick mother.
~ Defence Lawyer (1965-)

Workshop, they said.

And I thought it was just another place where they teach the inmates to earn a living when they cease to be inmates, like the Book Room or the Tailoring Room or even the Class Room, a high-ceilinged hall with broken furniture piled in one corner, where a few inmates, some of them well past their prime, prepare themselves to write high-school exams. But it turned out to be none of those places, but a bunch of smiling men who sat behind desks the wardens had us haul out to the courtyard and place under the gooseberry trees. They sat with their backs turned to a banner strung between two pillars. *You talk. We listen.*

In spite of the promise on the banner, they did most of the talking and we did the listening because the superintendent was leaning against a pillar, frowning at the glare of sunlight on the Record Room windows. At first they talked through the microphone, poking fun at each other for their receding hairlines, expanding waistlines and insatiable appetite as a way of introduction. I imagined their voices climbing over the bronze-coloured walls and floating along the highways they would themselves travel later in the day. Then they split us up into small groups as if we were about to be hung in batches, and talked to us one by one in near murmurs, like whispering the last prayers to us.

They already knew everything important about us: the nature of our crime, the length of our punishment, how long it would be before we walked free. They knew everything except the individual jailbreak plans we hid in the folds of our brains. The wardens must have let them peek into our records, into our past, into the blur of our future. What set them apart from the human rights officials and social activists, who visit prisons more frequently and earnestly than inmates' kin do, was their curiosity. It was a while before I realized it was their profession to be curious. They belonged to a research organization, and had been hired by a magazine to do a study on how captivity changed convicts' lives. Dumb topic. Does anyone speak the truth when their daily life is researched into? (Ammi once told a research lady we owned a Philips colour television when the truth was the imam had forbidden us from watching even the neighbours' TV. Which size, the research lady had asked. Fairly big, Ammi replied.)

Watching them talk, occasionally mocking each other over the public announcement system for their identical girth, I had a sudden brainwave, an intuition, which said there was something for me in these men in ties: a hidden possibility, a chance to dare, a flicker of hope. They would not allow me to be a stowaway in their van – of course not. Nor would they slip a packet of cigarettes into my hands when it was safe to do so – no way. But this band of smiling men did foreshadow an opportunity, the exact nature of which I had no clue about.

As specimens they preferred inmates who had got long terms to those whose time here was more or less up. That made me an easy candidate, and I found myself sitting in the spidery shade of a gooseberry tree with a man who looked intensely familiar from a distance but a complete stranger up close. His face lit up the moment he read out my name from a sheet of paper pinned to his clipboard, as if spending an afternoon with Imran Jabbari improved his prospects at the office.

'Imran bhai,' he said, tapping me lightly on the knee, as if he had known me from the other life, from happier days. There was so much gel in his hair that the sun seemed to slip off his head and fall onto his knees in tiny white circles. 'I am sure the past eighteen months have changed you a lot.'

The eighteen months had not changed me much, except for one thing: I had started seeing printed words where there were actually none. But that was not a change a research agency would accept as a significant change. So I shook my head, indicating a firm no.

He placed his hands on his knees, and warmed his palms on them. The white circles were now on the back of his hands. '11/11,' he sighed. 'Such a coincidence that all tragic days have an 11 to it, isn't?'

I didn't know about the other 11s. But 11/11 was no coincidence; it was how they wanted it, so that history would be easy to remember in numbers as simple as the multiplication table of one. No one goes wrong with the multiplication table of one. No one can.

'You were more than an average student in school. Then you dropped out.' He looked up from the file, absently turning a page. 'Why?'

I smiled with the corner of my mouth. So he knew I was not going to answer this question or any other question he might have up his sleeve. I, like many other inmates, was bearing with these Workshop men just because the superintendent was still watching us.

'You even wrote a story for the school magazine and when it was rejected you sprayed ink on the teacher who laughed at it. Am I right?'

Wrong. It was a poem, not a story, and I had copied it from my sister's English text and jumbled the words so it would look fresh and original. But I held my tongue; it no longer mattered if it was verse or prose, rejected or published, if I was punished for squirting ink on the English teacher's shirt or let off with a stern warning.

'Your father is a priest,' he read out from the file, as if I didn't know yet.

I nodded and he appeared relieved: I was finally responding to his research.

'Was he the type …' he stopped, hesitating over the next word, and then started drawing medium-sized breasts in the air with his forefinger. 'Was he the type of person who … who … let me put it this way … a person who would appreciate what the Al-Qaeda, Taliban and people like that do?'

One of the most respected personalities of Vanity Bagh, though a complete nonentity outside it, the imam had never been asked these kinds of uncivilized questions. If someone ever developed the nerve to question his integrity in this manner, he would have given that person a piece of his mind, a big chunk of it, in fact. In public the imam loathed violence, and preached what every other Muslim clergyman does when a human bomb kills enough people to make headlines: that peace is the religion of Islam. Not that he sympathized with the fidayeen in private. The only time he wanted to be a human bomb was when Ammi came back from Haja Stores on the eve of an Eid with too many shopping bags and a Chinese umbrella. He frowned at the bags and announced it was time he took Khomeini sahib's fatwa seriously and blew himself up when Rushdie was around so that Ammi and the rest of us could wallow in the same degree of luxury Mir sahib's wife and children were spoilt with. Anger spread on Ammi's face like a rash, and she ordered me to take the bags and the umbrella back to Haja Stores and get a refund. 'Give the money to your Abba. And tell him no one dies if he blows himself up. I am the living example.'

In Vanity Bagh, most shopkeepers treat young boys like beggars. Those who don't are either genuinely good at heart or plain paedophiles. Shahul Haja was neither, and he bluntly refused the refund on the grounds that I had no receipts to show. Bags piled on my forearms and the Chinese umbrella hanging from my shirt collar like a counterweight, I waddled home past Zia and his friends who made farting sounds with every step I took. (We went to different schools; we were not friends yet.) Ammi scowled at the sight of the bags she no longer wanted and shoved a screw of pulpy pink bills into my pocket. Zia and his friends farted with their lips when I picked my burdened way back to Haja Stores.

Here goes the boy again,
carrying the burden of life in his tender hands.
– The madwoman outside the masjid (-2007)

Hands laden with things nobody wanted to take immediate possession of, I requested the shopkeeper to dig into my trousers for the receipts, and his hand went so deep into my pocket that it nearly brushed my balls.

Bhenchod, what am I supposed to do
with your electricity bills?
– Shahul Haja Khan (1934–99)

Blind with rage, Ammi had given me the wrong bills. At the thought of having to brave Zia and the madwoman for the third time that afternoon, it was I who wanted to blow myself up into tiny pieces neither the imam nor Ammi could fix back even if they tried with Fevi Kwik or Araldite. All of a sudden I found the imam standing beside me and talking to Shahul Haja, who had swiftly loosened up and was offering to take the purchases back without proper receipts. The imam, on the other hand, was apologizing for the confusion and saying his wife had changed her mind again: she would now like to keep every piece of her afternoon shopping with her. 'These women,' he said, laughing. 'These women,' said Shahul Haja, laughing with the imam.

The Workshop man was rapping the end of his pen against the clipboard, the way animal trainers in the circus do while their dogs do sums on a blackboard, as if he could control my thoughts with codes thus relayed. Abruptly he stopped and, just as I was expecting him to heave a sigh and let go of me, he asked, 'What do they teach you at the madrasa?'

Since 11/11, I had been asked this question more often than I had been asked my name. During the interrogation and the trial and even during my first weeks here I heard this question asked, sometimes with serious interest, sometimes as a way of mocking, and I had only one answer no matter what tone of voice my interrogators chose to employ: *Madrasas teach you what they are supposed to: the Holy Quran*. And they all smiled in a bad way like I had told them a joke they had already heard.

'I am just being curious, Imran bhai,' the Workshop man said. The sun was glinting on the long strands of his hair plastered together by too much gel. I was getting a headache just by looking at it. 'How do you remember the madrasa you studied at?'

The only madrasa in Vanity Bagh is a long, shady verandah at the back of the mosque. The sun streams in through an expanse of reed curtains and falls softly on the cracked olive floor like a faded Persian carpet. There are benches but no desks, so the children spread their books on their laps and chant what they are instructed to. Behind the verandah is a square grassy patch where mullahs occasionally congregate under the willow tree and chat late into the night. Whenever Abu Hathim sahib pays a visit to the mosque, he never goes home without a laborious trip to the backyard, where he stands under the willow tree the same way a visiting dignitary does in front of a national memorial, chin dropped to the chest, eyes closed. Under the tree a potted dahlia sits on an almost unobtrusive mound of earth, over which he runs his fingers warily and then presses them against his lips.

Beneath the potted dahlia lies little Sinbad, Abu Hathim sahib's youngest and the most favourite grandchild. Four years ago Sinbad died at the age of seven in a car accident. There were rumours that the truck that hit the car was driven by a professional killer who had been hired to bump off Abu Hathim sahib's son. But on that fateful day it was the chauffeur who drove Sinbad to school; the truck killed the boy on the spot and the chauffeur died in a wailing ambulance. We were all shaken, especially the ladies. Sinbad was to be buried in Purana Masjid kabristan where Vanity Bagh buries its dead, but Abu Hathim sahib just couldn't let the boy leave his bungalow, let alone the mohalla. Some sentiments are so senseless that they make you angry. This one made the imam fume; he would have even shouted if it was anybody other than Abu Hathim sahib. No one shouts at Abu Hathim sahib. No one even dares hold his gaze for longer than a few seconds. After clearing his throat several times, the imam found his voice and tried to make Abu Hathim sahib see the point: it is utterly un-Islamic to bury the dead in private premises unless you are a Mogul ruler or your killer wants to hide your body. But Abu Hathim sahib never sees a point other than the ones he himself makes. Sinbad's father was willing to bury him anywhere. He even appealed to Abu Hathim sahib to comply with the Islamic rules. Impervious to such entreaties, which now came from everyone bold enough to speak up, the old man wouldn't let the body go. The imam sat stiffly next to Abu Hathim sahib with a finger pressed to the side of his head, apparently thinking about the next best option to facilitate an Islamic burial. Mourners started sniffing, glancing around; it was the same familiar sulphuric smell that pervaded our home when the imam broke wind. Abu Hathim sahib momentarily recovered from the delirium to sniff the air and look accusingly around, as if asking, 'Who dared do this in my house?' I ranked that as the top joke of 2006.

As the day wore on, Abu Hathim sahib showed signs of thawing. He said he would allow the boy to be buried behind the madrasa. But behind the madrasa there was only a small patch of land. 'There is enough room for my little Sinbad,' he groaned. 'And enough space for me beside him when I die.' It was very moving to watch a don cry.

There was nearly a stampede to carry the body. When the rich and the famous die everyone wants their share of involvement in the funeral. Even the boy's father and uncles got elbowed out, but I managed to hang on to a pole of the green casket. It was one of the biggest surprises of my life. The casket, though it was riding on how many hands only God knew, weighed like it had a little bull inside. Sinbad was a tiny boy even a one-legged person like Abu Hathim sahib used to carry with ease. I remember believing for a moment that in death the boy had amassed the weight of the sixty or so years he would have lived had the truck not rammed into the car. I had a glimpse of his face when the winding sheet was opened just before they placed six planks on his grave. He was smiling with the corner of his mouth: a mocking, frozen smile that is the official emoticon of the mohalla-wallahs when they wish to wordlessly disapprove of something. I could not sleep for the next two days. On the third day, Abu Hathim sahib stepped through the madrasa and placed a pot of green dahlias on the grave. Before that I had not known that dahlias could bear green flowers.

'You have been staring at that tree for the last ten minutes, Imran bhai,' the Workshop man said. 'And you haven't answered my question about the madrasa and the one before that.'

I closed my eyes and heard it rain, a rain that fell thirteen miles away behind the madrasa; I heard the clink of raindrops as the awning tiles of the mosque dripped onto the ablution tank. Through the sound of rain I heard a papery voice, which said in a tone of indifference I never knew I was capable of producing, 'There is a willow tree behind the madrasa.'

'Willow tree? Really?' the Workshop man asked, and I opened my eyes. The sun in the prison yard was many shades fiercer than the mellow light that graced the alleys of Vanity Bagh. There was surprise on the face of the Workshop man as if a willow tree had been in one of his recent dreams. 'And I guess you miss that tree. Right?'

'There is a pot of dahlias under the tree.' My voice was less papery this time, and more involved. 'The pot is placed there as a mark. There is a big secret buried under it.'

'What secret is buried under the pot?' he asked, beginning to frown.

Since I had been made to sit in front of this man whose gelled hair now reminded me of Mandrake, I had been plotting against him, whom I had met for the first time that morning, and his world, which I did not even have a faint mental picture of. Then, all of a sudden, I knew why I wanted to set this stranger up: I could not wait for fourteen odd years to be in Vanity Bagh again. I wanted to see the mohalla now, just once at least, just for a few hours, even for a few minutes. I considered it a mission accomplished if this man could be sent back to the real world with a false story. A story he would share with the magazine that had hired his group. A tiny speck of a story the magazine could blow into a big molten bubble. A story that would switch on a big spotlight over Vanity Bagh like in award shows and the circus. Look at the irony: a convict's story carries a lot of weight whereas an under trial's tale would always be met with a smirk. The world is a silly place. It can't help pettiness. So I decided to mislead him, the same way you mislead wailing police cars in computer games so that they would tip over riverbanks lined with fake 'Bridge Ahead' signs. I could already see the imam turn the leaves of the magazine without taking it off the newsstand.

'Tell me your little secret, Imran bhai,' the Workshop man pleaded, adding a smile to his words as an afterthought.

'There is a big crate of bombs buried under the pot.'

He looked across the yard where the superintendent stood admiring the tip of his shoes. Then he looked back at me, his Adam's apple moving slowly as he gulped. 'Are you sure?'

'I saw them bury the crate under the tree.'

'Who?'

'Abu Hathim and his sons.'

He puckered his lips into a brown rosebud and shook his head slightly for a long time, like a rubber doll made to rock in the lightest of breezes.

'But why are you telling me your little secret which is actually big?' he asked at length.

'Because I am a changed man now.'

The sudden light in his eyes, which he tried to hide from me by blinking, said he got much more than he had come looking for. He exhaled noisily and then extended a hand. My first handshake in a long time. I looked at the superintendent. The superintendent looked away. I shook the Workshop man's hand. A hand that would touch things that existed in the real world later in the day. 'Nice meeting you, Imran. I can see you are beginning to be a new man. Good going.'

I hurried to the Book Room, badly wanting to open an empty book and read from it. But the Book Room stood closed, padlocked. Then I remembered it was a Sunday. Sunday is a holiday. Even in prison.

V

I saw him in the parking lot, reading a movie poster.
I got suspicious, because nobody reads movie posters for real.

~ Witness No. 7 (-)

The Workshop man seemed to have kept the story to himself, for when Ammi paid her monthly visit last week she did not mention anything about the National Investigative Agency marching through the mosque and digging up what four years had reduced little Sinbad's body to. When the NIA first combed the mohalla soon after 11/11, hell had broken loose in Vanity Bagh, and the mohalla-wallahs had locked themselves in and decided to pretend they were not at home if the doorbell rang. The cleverer ones padlocked their doors from outside and sneaked back inside through the windows, as if a lock was enough to make the NIA turn on its heels and go home. Mogul Bakery stuck a hurriedly composed poster on its shutter announcing that the shop was closed for renovation. It reopened a few hours later upon news of our arrest, and the mohalla-wallahs threw their doors wide open and inhaled fresh air as word spread that the NIA had bundled Zia and me into a jeep and driven away, blazing headlights and blaring horns.

Had the NIA revisited the mohalla, Ammi would have talked about it with a lot of zeal and drama, without even the faintest suspicion that I was the one who had made it happen from here. Had the NIA been to the mohalla, she did not even have to tell me: news of Vanity Bagh's furious resistance or shameful submission would have penetrated even the barbed, brazen walls.

Just like the unlicenced cable TV studio that Sarfraz used to run from a dingy room behind Pintos' Garage, Ammi enlightens me on everything that happens in the mohalla in a fifteen-minute capsule that aligns deaths, divorces, pregnancies, childbirth, circumcisions, weddings and other little tragedies on a long straight line. She doesn't miss out on a single episode, however inconsequential. On the other hand, I take only a few minutes to tell her what happens here – nothing much happens here. She stares past me at the walls as I talk, probably imagining life in a prison once visiting hours are over and the prison regains its monochrome shades and monotonous sounds. I doubt if she can imagine the depth of despair that always overwhelms you when twilight dawns and there are no streetlamps flickering to life anywhere in sight. I suppose every inmate misses streetlights, and the flies that buzz around in their sad yellow vignettes.

Ammi's eyes brightened up a little when I told her about my new job in the Book Room, though the smile she gave me was similar to the one Sinbad smiled from his grave.

'Why did you smile?' I asked, suddenly angry.

'Because I am happy for you,' she said.

'But you didn't give me a happy smile. You gave me a different kind of smile.'

She shaped her lips in a bad attempt at a better smile. 'When you were in school, you never touched your books. Now you have to do that every day.'

How true! My love of books came rather late in life. In childhood my fascination for books was limited to the rexine-bound ledger the imam brought home on Friday nights. It had a shiny green cover, at the centre of which was a crescent Fatima had cut out from a magazine at the behest of the imam. Inside was the inky scrawl that could only have been jointly produced by the imam's ancient fountain pen and his shivering left hand. There was nothing interesting inside, just the unauthorized census of the mohalla, and the details of the quarterly donations Muslim households made to the masjid. If you looked at it closely, the way I did, you saw the rushed history of the street and the fluctuating fortunes of its people except the Pintos, half a dozen Sikh families and a few Jains. The imam brought the ledger home on Friday nights to update it from memory, to make amendments to its pages in accordance with the changes Allah had done in His ledger. In case of a death, he would record the year of demise against the name which would already have the year of birth next to it, and close the bracket. A case shut forever. In case of a birth, he would just scribble '+1' on the margin of the page dedicated to the blessed family, '+2' if it was twins.

I found the entries fascinating, and wondered about the expiry date of each of the mohalla-wallahs. My name is there, as are Wasim's, Ammi's and the imam's. Fatima's was struck out soon after she was married off. I sometimes wonder if the imam crossed out my name after 11/11, just to please the NIA if not for anything else.

When the visiting hours end with a long, rhythmic peal of an electric bell, Ammi promptly cries. Then she turns away without bidding goodbye and starts her journey home. I watch her pick her way along the beds of red spinach, around the Record Room, and disappear down the road that leads her into a world as crowded as cartoon strips. I too cry, but in an invisible way. I sit under one of the gooseberry trees and let unhappiness settle down to the bottom of my mind like silt. Only then do I return to what I have been interrupted from. But last time I skipped my usual stopover under the huddle of the gooseberry trees and headed straight back to the Book Room, where I grabbed a book from the worktable and stared at its empty pages with moist eyes. I saw the street Ammi was travelling to, I saw the light failing so rapidly over the mohalla that it would be dark by the time she got off the bus and walked past Franklin. I saw birds landing on the dark boughs, like the details from a nightmare the tree was going to have once the street went to bed.

Vanity Bagh, like many people who live in its poky lanes and blind alleys, has a nickname, which the rest of Mangobagh slapped on it like a parking ticket soon after Pakistan won the cricket world cup in 1992. I was just about seven then, groaning at the top of my voice that I was going to die. Ammi asked me to be quiet; no one had ever died of measles.

There are many versions of how the mohalla earned its nickname. But this is the most reliable and, in the light of our street's reputation, the most likely one. On the night of

Pakistan's world cup victory a minor fight erupted outside Khan Hair Salon, but belligerence never stays minor or moderate in Vanity Bagh; the unease quickly spread through the mohalla and even spilled onto Ashraf Bagh and Mehendi, escalating into a big riot by the next sunrise. I didn't sleep a wink that night; on the brink of falling asleep, I heard a window being smashed somewhere, and every half hour or so a gun fired, a bang that reassured us that the neighbourhood was still in safe hands, that Abu Hathim sahib was standing as tall as King Kong at the mouth of the street, holding fort. I even imagined a cavalcade of rioters trying to sneak past him through the space between his five-storey-high legs and he, the local guardian of all the mohalla-wallahs, squashing them under his feet to an unrecognizable mangle the way he crushed his country cheroots after a few puffs.

The riot was not our doing. The mohalla-wallahs hardly start a riot, though once dragged into it you need water cannons and teargas shells, sometimes even a few rounds of firing, to coax them back home. A band of hardcore Hindus from the railway quarters had started the trouble. They were riding through Vanity Bagh after their evening drill at the Ramleela Grounds (what were they getting trained for, anyway?) when Sharif Khan, a good batsman in addition to being an excellent barber, was lighting a long hank of firecrackers in celebration of the world cup victory. His friends and a few of his clients were doing a kind of fire dance on the sidewalk with green ribbons tied to their wrists as chain crackers went off like artillery. The last scooter in the convoy took a U-turn near Mogul Bakery and came back, halting near the salon as the last of the crackers popped off and all that remained of the celebration was a drifting cloud of smoke and the smell of gunpowder.

The alien wore a pair of khaki shorts and a white shirt; on his bony head sat a black cap which was not much different from what the imam wore for the Eid day speech, only that his was made of fur and the alien's of some cheaper, stiffer material.

'What are you celebrating?' Black Cap asked Sharif Khan.

Sharif Khan, who had no talent for answering unexpected questions, merely shrugged. And a shrug is always seen as a sign of weakness or indifference in every part of Mangobagh.

Your father is fucking dead or something?
– Black Cap (-1992)

When you made a reference to Sharif Khan's father, who had gone to Mumbai to act in the movies when Sharif Khan had been just a toddler and never come back, two things were certain to happen. First, a globule of spittle would land on your face. Then a tightly clenched fist would leave the bridge of your nose numb and bleeding.

Black Cap nursed his broken nose with a hanky, which suddenly developed red floral patterns on its folds. 'Brothers, come back,' he screamed to the disappearing bunch of scooters. In the roar of traffic, only his assailants heard him.

When you irked Sharif Khan, you irked his friends too, and they kicked Black Cap around the pavement like a football until the barber struck the pose of a referee ending the play, holding an authoritative hand up. Back in those days Khan Hair Salon was not a well-lit place, and the brawl happened in the dim light of the salon signboard. Later that night, though, Khan Hair Salon became the brightest spot in the whole of Vanity Bagh as it went up in flames, blazing with a determination even water and sand could not douse. By the time a fire engine could reach the street all that remained of the salon was a charred barber's chair, which was swivelling of its own accord as if a spirit were sitting on it and admiring its new haircut in the blackened mirror. Barely an hour had passed when the legendary riot manager of Vanity Bagh parked his vintage car under Franklin and scaled its roof, and called for collective action.

Time for jihad has come, bhaion.
Pledge to kill every kafir you see. Bolo Takbir …
– Jalal 'Jihadi' Ahmed (1935-1992)

Allahu Akbar …
– Jamsheer 'Jihadi' Ahmed (1973-1992)

The mohalla-wallahs took a two-hour break from rioting to bury Jalal Ahmed sahib and his youngest son Jamsheer side by side in the kabristan behind Purana Masjid. After throwing dust into the twin graves they rushed back to the street and resumed the campaign with renewed vengeance, wielding freshly stropped weaponry.

Raids succeeded the riots, and the imam was worried sick about the machete that he always kept under his bed, which he thought would compensate for our flimsy front door. He had brought the machete home the day Fatima had formally become a woman and Ammi had banned her from leaving home without purdah. The imam considered hiding it behind a rafter and was mounting a stool when the police thumped on our door.

'You can come in,' the imam told the inspector in a priestly voice as he stood blocking the way. 'But one of my boys is down with chickenpox.'

At the mention of chickenpox, though I had only measles, the inspector froze at the doorway and bit his lip in serious indecision, while Fatima whispered to me to groan as if the boils on my body were plopping off like the units in bubble wrap.

'Not a problem,' we heard the inspector say after a while. 'We have had chickenpox at some stage of our lives. So, no worries.'

'I'm the chief imam of Masjid-e-Mosavi.' He sounded as if he had developed a sore throat all of a sudden.

'All the more reason to search this place,' the inspector said, treading into the house with a small regiment of policemen who smelt of quelled fire. Frightened by the sound of boots, Wasim climbed onto Fatima's hips and sat there whimpering till the house was free of intruders again.

'Were you among the people celebrating on the street last night?' the inspector asked, lifting a table cover with the end of his baton.

'No,' the imam said in a hurt voice. 'No way.'

'Any idea who all were celebrating Pakistan's victory? I want some prominent names.'

'I don't know,' the imam replied readily, defiantly. 'And I don't know why you interpret it as a celebration of Pakistan's victory. Couldn't they have been celebrating the defeat of England who ruled us for so many years?'

An unexpected peal of laughter erupted from the inspector, and when it stopped as abruptly as it had started, he wiped tears from the corners of his eyes and gestured at the policemen to start the search. The way the policemen moved about the house suggested that they had been instructed not to ill-treat the imam until the raid unearthed something that linked him to the riots: a can of petrol, a nip of gunpowder, a bunch of sticks, a machete …

Machete! If the imam was not already in a soup he was treading the rim of the bowl, tumbling over any time now. Never a good actor, he made a disastrous attempt to look unruffled, but his eyes kept returning to the spot where he had thought of hiding the machete but didn't have the time to. The inspector stood with his back turned to a window, watching the imam from the corner of his eye while turning the pages of Fatima's science reader. After a long scrutiny he put the reader back on the windowsill and climbed a chair without even taking off his shoes. He groped behind the rafter from which the imam could not peel his eyes off, but all his search yielded were stringy pieces of cobweb that fell on his face.

'Fatima,' the imam said. 'Get some ice water from the fridge for inspector sir. He needs to wash his face.'

We never had a fridge. The imam was just poking fun at the inspector, knowing which Fatima neither went to the kitchen nor asked the inspector if he would settle for plain pipe water. The policemen who had charged into the kitchen found a tall woman squatting on the floor, doubled up over a long knife which she kept pressed to the ground by her toes. She was so involvedly slicing vegetables against its glistening blade that the policemen thought it rude to interrupt her. They quietly poked their lathis at the mounds of ash in the hearth while she ran chunks of snake gourd through the long blade of the kitchen knife. They opened old tins of Cerelac and sniffed at the condiments stored inside while she started to chop green mangoes. After a while they came out of the kitchen on the verge of a sneeze, and shook their heads solemnly at the inspector.

'Bathe the boy in turmeric water. It is good for chickenpox marks,' the inspector told Fatima before leading his men out into the alley. Once the sound of boots faded away to the street, interspersed with the squeals of chickens that flew off the alley to escape being kicked, Ammi brought the machete back to the front room, wiping its blade with her dupatta. 'Here is the sword of Tipu Sultan.'

'My missus is a little genie,' the imam said proudly.

'It's not genie, Abba,' Fatima cried through her titters. 'What you mean is genius.' She ranked it as the top joke of 1992.

The riots fizzled out in two days, the raids took one more day to die down, but it would be another three months before Khan Hair Salon would bear a resemblance to what it had been prior to Pakistan's world cup victory. It had irrevocably lost its cowboy-salon look – the new swing doors and fanlights failed to reconstruct the old charm – but the salon had found a new glory, for the simple reason that it had found Vanity Bagh a new name: Little Pakistan.

The elderly of the Khan clan found it hard to stop exaggerating their agony on the days of the riots and raids; the younger ones, on the other hand, simply chose to brag.

In the madrasa, where we yelled verses from the Quran like slogans during weekends, where the imam had once flogged me with forced anger for addressing him as 'Abba' (he later took me to Mogul Bakery and said he just wanted to convey to the class that I enjoyed no special privileges as his son), in the madrasa Sharif Khan's youngest son Navaz told us many hard-to-believe stories. The worst one was about a Pakistani leader writing to his father to congratulate him on his valour and to invite him to Karachi in case he should ever flee Vanity Bagh. We all knew there was no postal service between India and Pakistan, and nobody big would stoop so low as to write to a barber like Sharif Khan. But we never laughed at his stories, for we wanted to hear more of them. Then one day someone borrowed his copy of the Quran and discovered that he had made small yet significant modifications to his name, had turned it into a worldlier one. Striking out the name he had so pompously uttered on our first day at the madrasa, he had more pompously etched the new one; and the change from Navas Khan to Navaz Sharif was borne in silence. Just like his stories. Years later, when we formed the gang and he became one of the six members, we realized that none among us had a more Pakistani name than his.

A warden who has been watching me hold the same book for some time is finally coming over to probe. Let me quickly put the feather between the pages and close the book. I promise more reading on another day. Till then.

VI

Send me home, Judge sahib,
send me home. Or hang me.
~ Zia-ul-Haq (1984-2012)

Everyone dreams of jailbreak. Even people who have never been jailed do. The only exception is Frank Leone in *Lock Up*, which happens entirely in a jail except when Frank Leone and his love stroll hand in hand as snow falls on them like marshmallow puffs. But that is just flashback, and flashback is the most inevitable and important thing to happen to prisoners, in movies and in real life. The jail Frank Leone is in has a huge, ugly door but the rest of it is tastefully done. It is so beautiful in wide angle that you think the prisoners get there through a raffle.

(A good cinematographer can make anything look inviting; that is why all the young people who grow up watching noon shows at Kemps, Zeenat's and Central Plaza want to dump their parents and go to America. In his heart of hearts Wasim wants to do that too, though he knows his chances are grim.

First, refrigeration is not a much-in-demand-profession in a cold place like America. Second, after 9/11 Muslims are not welcome in America even if you are the best computer expert or physiotherapist in town. If they could strip people like Abdul Kalam and Shah Rukh Khan at airports, what chances does Wasim stand? They would happily send a spear up his rectum and plant him inside a police museum. A suspect from India. Stuffed for you.)

We ranked *Lock Up* as the top movie of 2005, though it was already an old movie. If there were Oscars for jailbreak scenes alone, it would have won every single one of them. And the dialogues – they made me stare at the mirror and imitate the man who uttered them on screen.

> I don't have to prove nothing.
> I came here for an execution.
> – Sylvester Stallone (1946–)

We watched it for the first time in the summer of 2005. Those days we used to watch one English movie per night on the DVD player in Khan Hair Salon (and a barber's chair gives you a much better recline than the seats these multiplexes charge you a bomb for). When I watched *Lock Up* for the first time or the second time or the twentieth time, little did I know that I would ever see the interior of a prison, let alone languish behind its copper-coloured walls. The DVD had been sitting on the half-price rack of Abid Videos for years before Jinnah took a serious interest in the title and shoplifted it. In the movie, according to Urdu subtitles, Stallone is not a compulsive jail-jumper; he handles hardships with a level of composure he exhibited neither in *First Blood* nor in *Rambo*. But the superintendent, for reasons even subtitles cannot adequately convey, is hell-bent on making Stallone break the law so that he could lock him up for the rest of the movie. We have a much more straightforward superintendent in comparison. Ours doesn't plot even for timepass. I do.

I always plan my jailbreak around a day of national importance – Republic Day or Independence Day – when everyone is busy wrapping silver foil around tree trunks or hanging streamers in the courtyard or leaning over tables arranged in a long line behind the kitchen, chopping vegetables for the special midday meal. In my plans I am armed with a steely resolve and the necessary accessories: a knife, a coil of rope and a can of deodorant. The knife is for self-defence, rope for scaling the mossy wall behind the disused Death Room. Deodorant kills the odour of sweat and leaves sniffer dogs all fucked up – if it doesn't I can accuse Rexona of misleading prisoners with their commercial.

At the back of the prison stand trees that are tall enough to have their tops sticking above the high walls. I don't know what else awaits me beyond the back wall. I picture a tiny house nestling among coconut palms and chikoo trees, a house whose sole purpose is to help me shed the prison clothes and acquire a civilian outfit. I can even see shades of clothes waiting to be stolen on a flagging laundry line. Blue denims and an olive tank top. Even a white cap with 'Green Mangobagh Clean Mangobagh' sewed onto its pea-green visor. Thus dressed in clothes smelling of sunshine and starch, I would tear through the woods, not looking back, not going to stop for the rest of my term if footfalls follow me down the carpet of sepia leaves.

Since my appointment in the Book Room, which has equipped me with this rare ability to read from blank pages, I make fewer plans for a jailbreak.

A good book is a great escape.
– Shair Shoukath (1928-2010)

A blank book is as good as a jailbreak.
– Imran Jabbari (1985-)

The moment I open a book, its covers still spongy from clumsy gumming, the whole mohalla springs up from the pages like the pop-up stable in a Christmas card. I look around. In a patch of the summer sun a warden with a horseshoe moustache sinks deeper into his chair and closes his eyes slowly, like dying people in movies do. I open my eyes wide and start reading from pages that have never been written on.

If Vanity Bagh is a pocket-sized Pakistan, it is only natural to have the Line of Control, however tenuous, running through some part of Mangobagh. The invisible LoC cuts through the old city, diagonally north of the mohalla, just three miles from the Char Bazaar intersection. Our territory ends abruptly on the brink of Broadway. Beyond that, a couple of blocks after the Air India building, the road becomes narrow, lined with apartment blocks that have the same weathered faces on which half-open ventilators sit like sleepy eyes. This neighbourhood is called Mehendi, a rambling Hindu colony which celebrates every festival with saffron flags and yolk-coloured laddoos. The mohalla-wallahs rarely venture beyond the Air India building, and on the rare occasions they have to, they do so after discreetly hiding their Muslim identities and idiosyncrasies.

When Mogul Bakery started advertising its free home delivery service in *Hello Evening*, Mehendi developed an instant appetite for Vanity Bagh's famed mutton patties, but every time it placed an order, small or big, Mir sahib apologized for the service being temporarily suspended for want of delivery boys and flung the order out of the window, swearing under his breath.

Since the Partition, Vanity Bagh has been at constant war with Mehendi, though the riots following Pakistan's world cup victory (or England's world cup defeat, as the imam would put it) had given the enmity a new dimension that even the upheavals of 1947 could not bring about. The Black Caps stopped passing through the mohalla after their evening drill at the Ramleela Grounds. Instead they took the roundabout way home, sticking to the highway and bearing with many bottlenecks. The overcautious White Caps ceased visiting Murgi Bazaar which lay too close to Mehendi to facilitate endless, shameless haggling sessions in its dingy lanes. So imagine our horror when the maiden operation for 5½ Men demanded us to be at the heart of this forbidden zone, that too in the dead of night when Mehendi seemed to lurk behind pillars to pounce on the very idea of Islam.

Our gang had been suffering from the same crisis that all clandestine businesses face at some stage of their evolution: obscurity. Even in our own mohalla we were completely unknown for obvious reasons; we couldn't possibly put advertisements in *Hello Evening* like Mogul Bakery did for its home delivery service, nor could we stand at a street corner and distribute handbills like Sharif Khan did for his salon. The only promotion we could afford and rely on was word of mouth, but we simply didn't know how to get people talking about a gang that dreamed of covert and mortal combats. Hamstrung by the lack of a sound promotional strategy, we were idling our time away by Franklin when we abruptly got hired. It still remains a mystery as to how our first client had come to know about us. He was a small-time pawnbroker who ran his business from a poky lane of Broadway, a venture we didn't even know existed until he rang up Navaz Sharif on his mobile phone one evening and said an eve-teasing type of hello.

'What can I do for you, sir?' Navaz Sharif asked like a helpline voice, only more sincerely. He was briefed sketchily over the phone about the job and the next evening, in the pawnbroker's cubicle made of sand-coloured plywood and opaque glass, Navaz Sharif and I were spoken to in great detail about the operation.

It appeared to be a job too simple to require six enthusiastic minds and as many pairs of quick hands, but then the pawnbroker did not know the strength of our gang and the extent of our genius. He never cared; all that concerned him was a neat, foolproof operation. He insisted that it was a simple job. We were to track down a second-hand Toyota Corolla he had financed and his client had vanished with; we were to seize it by force or by deceit and bring it to the recovery yard behind the Purana Masjid kabristan. Khatam, he had said. You are done.

Everything looked perfect, even familiar, like a scene from a movie we had watched long ago and remembered only in patches, until he gave us the address. Navaz Sharif and I howled in unison, as if we had just seen what Yahya had claimed to have witnessed quite a few times – Iskander's ghost moving behind the public lavatory window.

But we could not dismiss the opportunity the way Mir sahib chucked the orders from Mehendi out of his shop. The world gives novices lesser chances, and we were still on the periphery of a world we reckoned to be big but didn't know the exact dimensions of. We stepped out of the sand-coloured office undecided, promising to be in touch by the next evening.

The imam tapped a bunch of keys on the window frame when the stairway got noisy with debates. There were many reasons we should not take the job. Then there were as many proverbs that suggested we grab it. Yahya kept on miming one, pointing a finger at the night sky, at the Almighty and then stabbing it on his chest thrice, indicating bravery of the highest order; maybe he wanted to shout in our faces 'Fortune favours the brave' or some equivalent he had silently picked up. The next evening Navaz Sharif called the pawnbroker to say yes, and Yahya attributed our decision to his immense powers of persuasion.

Soon after the 2.30 Charminar Express rumbled through the snoring mohalla, we set out for Mehendi. The moon was out and, for some strange reason, I thought of Benazir with a longing as we tiptoed past Mogul Bakery. Except for the winking reflection of a neon signage, her window was dark –

she had been married and gone from Vanity Bagh for nearly a year now.

Imran, we will have as many children
as the other Benazir. No?
– Benazir (1985-)

Other than a small kit containing screwdrivers, spanners, a pen torch and a foldable knife, we carried six Hindu names just in case we got caught. Our real names would have made us more than gangsters; in a place like Mehendi, at such an unearthly hour, a gang hailing from Vanity Bagh could be dubbed not only as the enemy of the neighbourhood but of the entire nation.

My name was C. Ganesh (C for circumcised) and I remember smuggling Wasim's *Easy Ways of Refrigeration* out of home, and a ridiculous story to go with it (I was somehow certain we were going to get caught): *I, Ganesh from 2nd Street Raja Mata Nagar, missed the suburban train from Parade Circle after my crash course on refrigeration. Sorry for passing through your area so late at night. Good night.* I kept the textbook tucked under my shirt, and the story of missing the train inside my head.

At intersections orange lights blinked at us, as if warning us not to venture beyond the Air India building. They appeared to tell us not to follow Abu Hathim sahib's footsteps simply because we were not cut out for a life of blockbuster description.

In our schooldays, the Air India building used to be the tallest structure in Mangobagh, visible from as far away as Fouji Bagh which lies across the Moosa River and has of late shrunk to the status of a flea market as business moved from this old garrison to the newer city. When our cousins visited from villages and mid-sized towns, we sat them on the crossbars of our bicycles and rode them down a warren of alleys until we were at the back of Loyola Park, over which the white structure loomed like a single block of ice twinkling in the sun. 'See,' we would shout proudly, proprietarily, 'the tallest building in the world.'

The white tiles on the building had long gone grey and ceased to gleam, and the cyclone of 2001 had left the huge neon sign atop the fourteenth floor seriously lopsided, so that the archer in the Air India logo now aimed his arrow at pedestrians. To dwarf it further in altitude and arrogance, three taller buildings had come up in a radius of two kilometres in just four years: two were malls, the third the headquarters of a software firm. Lured by the various attractions Mangobagh offered, the cousins continued to show up, but they were too grown-up now for crossbars and too informed to be fooled with superlatives; they went to the malls on their own and got themselves photographed against the Blackberry, Blueberry and Burberry roll-ups.

On foot it took us about twenty minutes to gain the first view of the Air India building: a glimpse of its red, blinking signage through treetops. In another five minutes we were directly under it. Though it looked anything but magnificent, the building in grandeur was still the most imposing architecture among a sea of waiting-to-collapse-in-a-drizzle structures that stretched from Ashraf Bagh to Mehendi. A lone light shone at a ninth-floor window; a few floors above it, perched on the roof at an angle, the much depleted neon sign trembled like a dying butterfly. Along the railing we tiptoed like a group meditating over hijacking the Air India office and flying it to a friendly destination.

Then we stopped. Mehendi stretched in front of us, washed in the moonlight, waiting to prey.

'Walk close to the buildings,' Zia whispered. 'And walk singly. Imran, you go first.'

As I crossed the intersection to the forbidden neighbourhood, my stomach started churning behind Wasim's refrigeration manual. The rest of the gang had stayed back on the safer side of the intersection, waiting to see if dogs leaped at me or torches were shone on my face. When nothing happened, they slipped into Mehendi one by one. I walked quieter than a cat. For me, such craftiness was chiselled to perfection at home where you had to be extra careful to sneak past the imam, who slept light and groped under the cot for the machete even if a curtain stirred louder than it was supposed to, and I had not woken him even once from his dreams, which he claimed to be always about hajj pilgrimages. On the pavement of Mehendi, dead leaves flattened under my heels without so much as a crackle, but those who followed me didn't have such a discreet way with their feet. Their footsteps sounded like a pack of children crunching away on a carton of Cadbury Perk. The other audible sound was the faint jingle of tools Jinnah carried in his kit.

Look for a black Toyota Corolla.
Number is MD-02-2997.
– Navaz Sharif (1982-2009)

Tracking the car down was simpler than spotting an

elephant from a cavalry. A neighbourhood marginally richer than ours, Mehendi gets about in small cars while Vanity Bagh is predominantly a two-wheeler community. After retrieving important papers for safekeeping, Mehendi leaves its cars on the street for the night, the entrances to old apartments lining the road being too narrow to let even a rickshaw through.

'There she is,' Navaz Sharif said. He classified anything without a dick as a woman. The black Corolla stood out arrogantly from a long line of smaller cars parked under a salt tree, the moon glinting on its roof.

'Let's get started, boys,' Zulfikar murmured, suddenly assuming the role of a leader.

It was under the salt tree that I realized the skills our parents had made us acquire had amply prepared us for a profession they wouldn't have approved of. After dropping out of school, Jinnah had spent a year at his uncle's one-room factory, where he had been supposed to learn making keys. But he learned more about picking locks than moulding keys. And here, on the main street of Mehendi, he stood on his knees by the moonlit Corolla, as if praying for world peace, and tampered with its door.

The lock put up a brave front for a few minutes, then succumbed to his advances with a crisp snap. The door fell open, and a heady stench of damp carpet and old leather wafted out. Jinnah started sneezing.

'Shut up,' snapped Zulfikar, easing himself into the car. He was the only one among us who could drive a car and mend it too; he had apprenticed at Pintos' Garage until the day he lost his temper and George Pinto a client. On getting sacked he hurled a spanner at George Pinto and walked out, his chest puffed out with fake pride.

> I'm cursing you. Your hands will tremble
> at the sight of a spanner. God bless you.
> – George Pinto (1951-   )

'Get in, boys,' Zulfikar whispered. 'Let's go.' Settling into the driver's seat, he flipped the sun visor, expecting a bunch of keys to tumble into his hands like they do in English movies. No keys; that gave him a chance to imitate a keyless Tom Cruise. Yanking two wires from under the steering wheel, he flicked their ends against each other like a caveman trying to work up a fire with stones. Much to everyone's surprise, the car roared into life and throbbed impatiently. 'Get in, all of you.'

Out of habit we slammed the doors shut, then looked apologetically at each other. But Mehendi seemed to be in a deeper slumber than the bang of car doors could wake it from. An adventure can't be this simple, I thought. How can an operation be complete without hiccups, hiding and hearts skipping a few beats? This was only a slightly upgraded version of stealing money from the imam's jubbahs.

The very next moment my conclusions were to be proved premature, and the operation was to go through all the phases I had envisaged essential for giving it a sense of completion.

The hiccup phase, to start with. We were about to roll away when the hollow boom of a motorbike floated down the street. For a minute it seemed that the motorbike was riding away from Mehendi, headed for Broadway or Ashraf Bagh, but soon we saw a circle of light appear near the Air India building. Zulfikar switched off the engine and signalled us to be quiet while the circle grew bigger and the motorbike came to a halt under a lamppost across the road from the Corolla. It was the kind of bike that looked good and muscular in magazines, but exactly like a trodden-over grasshopper on the road, with long, curving handlebars and an oval headlight. The light went off, and the pillion rider got off the bike.

The hiding phase, next. 'Quiet,' Zulfikar hissed. His face had gone pale, his voice shaky. I made sure Wasim's textbook was under my shirt, as if it were my bulletproof vest. Knowing that a fit of sneezing would change our lives forever, Jinnah caged his nose in his cupped hands and sat staring at a doll dangling from the rearview mirror.

The heart-missing-a-beat phase, to wind up. We sat still, staring into the distance, like a bereaved family, while the man on the bike lit a cigarette and exhaled blue smoke. His companion, a younger man in a tight T-shirt with very short sleeves, was leaning on a lamppost, his hands held behind the post like he was tethered to it and awaiting lashes. We would not have been surprised if they turned out to be Mehendi's night guards, men who had volunteered to save their street from Muslims, and were to spend the night chatting until the moon paled out and the sun rose at the end of an alleyway. But having finished his cigarette the man got off the bike and stood by the lamppost, hands on his hips, and surveyed the row of cars parked neatly along the road. His gaze froze on the Corolla for a moment, and I saw Zulfikar's hands reach out for the wires, ready to spark off a quick escape if he took a step towards us. What I saw next I have never seen again in my life. The man peeled his companion off the lamppost and, wrapping his hands around the young man's waist, kissed him on the mouth. A long, tender kiss.

'Lesbos,' Navaz Sharif whispered.

'Gays,' Zia panted. 'Gays.'

'Ass bumpers,' Jinnah said. 'And they have 101 jokes about Muslims doing that.'

The kisser and the kissed freed themselves from the tangle of hands at the blare of a train in the distance (probably the same train I had thought of cooking up a story about missing if caught by the men of Mehendi). A short while later they bid each other a silent goodbye: straddling the bike, the kisser launched a flying kiss; leaning against the lamppost, the kissed held his hand stiffly by his side, palm facing the ground, and waved curtly at his own feet. When the throbs of the bike faded down the street to the other end of Mehendi, the kissed started walking towards an alley, wiping his lips with the back of his hand.

'Sir Yahya has got an erection,' Jinnah started to titter.

'Shhhh …' Zulfikar hissed, flicking the ends of two wires against each other till the engine roared to life. With nothing more to witness, we steered out of Mehendi and cruised through Mangobagh, which didn't look like a city but an unending backyard lit by a huge yet pale night lamp.

VII

That is not my brother's blueprint for the 11/11 blast.
That is my half-yearly college project.
~ Wasim Jabbari (1988-)

Zia is very talented. He can shell up to six coconuts inside a minute. And he does not need a machete or an axe for that. His teeth would do a neater job in lesser time. Crazy stuff. I can't shell even a single one; even watching Zia do it sets my teeth on edge. I hope someone will have the guts to walk up to the superintendent and enlighten him on this wonderful skill Zia has. On second thought, I hope not. The superintendent might force the wardens to believe that Zia can gnaw away iron bars as well and disappear.

I met Zia yesterday after what seemed to be a couple of decades, though we both have been here for just about eighteen months. He lives only two blocks away, but he might as well have been living in Guantanamo. Rules are strict. Inter-block contact is not permitted, except on days of national importance when the prison is a borderless gathering in the courtyard; even then you cannot escape the cameras staring at you from pillars. (But you can blind a camera with a Big Babol. If you have six Big Babols and enough guts, you can leave the cameras useless and sneak out of the courtyard. Once out of the courtyard, getting as far as the wall behind the Death Room is child's play; beyond that it is an altogether different game, and everything depends on individual skills – climbing, jumping, sprinting, vanishing into thin air, everything.)

Yesterday I met Zia thanks to a little mishap. A fire broke out in the kitchen that serves E-Block and spread to the kitchen that serves F-Block, and both had to be shut down; so our kitchen was burdened with the task of feeding the entire prison. My suspicion is that the inmates in charge of the kitchens had wanted to start a fire big enough to make the wardens throw open the prison gates and order the entire jail out of the premises. But all it took to thwart a possible jailbreak plot were two fire extinguishers which had been hanging on the Record Room wall like something waiting to explode.

Queues stretched through trees like anacondas, and there were long delays and much caterwauling; some inmates were even clanking tumblers against plates as if they were revolting in a movie in which bad guys ruled the prison. When the superintendent came to have a sample morsel (yes, he tastes everything before we do, just like Ammi used to do when we were children, though he doesn't blow at piping-hot stuff like Ammi used to), a hush descended on the premises. He was, understandably, livid. With fake admiration for the ones who had whistled and yowled, he stood under a tree, wordlessly challenging the whistlers for an encore. No one whistled. No one so much as breathed audibly.

They had put the serving counters in opposite directions, so the queues passed each other like slow trains. Some stared at you, some smiled in a small way, just like people do when one train passes another. I did neither at Zia. I just winked. He, after a slight hesitation, winked back. There was enough time for a few words, but there were two wardens watching us.

Later in the Book Room, by the mere act of opening a book, I saw Zia on the night of our trip to Mehendi to impound the Corolla.

Zia speaking, sir. Operation success.
– Zia-ul-Haq (1984-2012)

Okay, okay. Don't say anything more on the phone.
Meet me in my office tomorrow.
– Pawnbroker (-)

After parking the car behind an abandoned fire station, we cut through gullies that smelled of sheep until we reached a part of the expressway that skirted the backside of Jumbo Cements Complex. In the distance, swathed in the moist light of sodium vapours, stood plants that made cement which, when converted into a commercial and aired on television, promised to bond life, not bricks or flint. Just as we passed the arched gateway of the factory the two o'clock siren blared, and workers poured out of the tall gates like impatient schoolchildren. The imam's younger brother worked in one of those plants; he worked in the fly ash unit and always wore a yolk yellow helmet, even when he went to the market or the ration shop on his off days, as if he dreaded the impact of an explosion would reach him even if he was miles away from the plant. But he did not work in the shift that ended at two o'clock, so I had no worries of confronting him.

Yahya mimed he was hungry, drawing an elaborate dinner in the air with his fingers. Along the factory wall were small but well-lit food stalls, and we ate from one of them, sitting amidst workers who had cement dust clinging to their bodies, which made them look like children who played all night in the hills of Horlicks. Although I had not had a proper mouthful since afternoon, I was not even remotely hungry. Maybe it was the refrigeration manual tucked under my shirt that made my tummy feel full. After eating we headed home down the expressway, throwing away our Hindu names like counterfoils we had no more use of.

Except for stray automobiles, the Iron Bridge was deserted. Halfway down the bridge we were stopped by the designs the moon had fashioned with the century-old girders. Across the asphalt porous shadows lay in pale lattice patterns. Down on the Moosa River the moon was a huge silver coin bleeding luminous ripples downstream. Navaz Sharif whipped out his two-megapixel mobile phone and started taking pictures. We posed against railings, hugged no-parking signs, leaned on stacks of traffic cones. We shaped Vs with our index and middle fingers, hung our tongues out, faked orgasms. While we struck poses of jamboree, Jinnah, the born graffiti maker, fished out his penknife and started to carve the name of our gang on a girder. A car slowed down and its windows were rolled down just as Navaz Sharif was making Zia and Yahya imitate the gays from Mehendi. Disrupted, Yahya blew the driver a flying kiss while Zia offered to donate his private parts to two old men in the backseat. The windows went up, the car went reluctantly away and Zulfikar warned us that somebody might already be dialling the police. We decided to split, after ranking it as what it deserved to be: the most memorable night of 2007.

Sneaking back home was a tougher task than slinking out of Mehendi with the Corolla. The imam, who looked on the verge of falling asleep during the day, was always on the brink of waking up at night; he had developed the habit of sleeping late and light for two reasons. The first – Fatima's formal initiation into womanhood – had long been rendered redundant by her marriage. The second was a hole in Wasim's heart, of which the imam had many x-ray images, which he stared dolefully at when Wasim was away at the refrigeration training centre.

I rated Wasim as a disappointing young man. It was a personal rating. 5½ Men never rated the families of its members. It was our corporate policy, though an unspoken one.

On some nights Wasim, so tall and frail he looked like Iskander's ghost passing through our house, paced the room which is only slightly more spacious than my cell. A hand on his chest, a light whistle on his breath, Wasim would appear seriously lovelorn, humming a tune for his sweetheart. And the imam, ever alert to signals of distress, would burst into the room no sooner than Wasim had started his restless trips between the narrow beds. Wasim had always been his pet, but a lesser pet in the days prior to him fainting in the class and being rushed to the hospital in an auto rickshaw, I wailing by his side.

In the middle of every month, except for the holy month

of Ramzan, Wasim had a relapse. He would rouse from the bed at small hours and stay restless until the imam nursed him back to some degree of wellness with a tiny pill and a few verses from the Quran dispensed to his ear in a whispery hiss. On occasions when the pill and the prayers failed to have any palliative effect on him, I was sent to fetch a taxi. The taxi rank near Mogul Bakery went empty much before midnight. On lucky nights I flagged down an auto rickshaw bumping through the mohalla. Else I hired one of the cycle rickshaws parked under Franklin, the rickshaw-wallah sleeping on the backseat with his knees drawn to his chest to make himself fit into the narrow space. I remember a night when the street didn't offer even this humblest means of transportation; I thought of calling one of my friends for help, but did not know how the imam would react to it as he strongly disapproved of all four-and-a-half of my friends. What else to do than wave frenziedly at approaching headlights as the imam struggled to keep Wasim on his feet on the sidewalk? Finally, a mini truck carrying fish to Begum Bazaar pulled up and carted us to the nearest hospital, the imam and Wasim travelling inside the driver's cabin, I on the tray of the truck, my feet planted in a sea of dead salmon. For three days afterwards, people started sniffing when I was around, in spite of me working a solid bar of Lifebuoy on my feet until it turned to a spongy little blob.

When I had to slink out of home and sneak back into it my bedside window served as the gateway. It opened to a narrow path running alongside Abbas Chacha's house, and led to the back of the shed where the imam parked his Hercules and Ammi tethered her two lambs, Tabu and Humera – the brown one named after an Indian actress, the white a Pakistani singer. Tabu let out a long, quavering bleat whenever she detected suspicious activity near the shed; that way Tabu was a dog. I once tried feeding her Big Babol so she would stop bleating. No such luck. She detested bubblegum.

Every time I regained entry into the house after a trip to Mangobagh's underbelly, I instructed myself to be quiet and cautious. A false step and the imam would be in the room, the pill in his hand, the prayer on his lips. Tabu had still not stopped bleating when I climbed over the sill and got into bed like an acrobat in slow motion. Wasim was in good health that night, and slept with his hands tucked between his legs. The moment I closed the window the room was filled with the smell of the Corolla we had steered down the backyard of Mangobagh to the recovery yard behind the kabristan.

The car continued to be in motion in my sleep, tearing through the heart of the city then sliding past unending stretches of parrot green cane fields, chased by police cars that had leapt straight out of *Transporter 1*. Beeps from Wasim's alarm clock broke the rhythm of this blurry grand prix once and, maybe an hour or so later, I heard him ask if anybody had seen one of his textbooks.

Jerome Pinto, who used to hang out with us till his father threatened to lock him up for the rest of his life and feed him three square meals a day through a window, once said that the best thing about being Christian was you could do bad things knowing they were bad, step into a tiny booth knowing you were going to be forgiven, confess everything to Father José or Father Rosario knowing they would never spill the beans, and step out feeling considerably less guilty.

Yours is a great religion, Junior Pinto.
– Muhammad Ali Jinnah (1983-2009)

Not being Christian, we sat on the steps of the mosque and merely rambled on until the adventure lost its sheen and our laughter its edge, and the imam knocked a bunch of keys menacingly against the window frame.

The pawnbroker had promptly paid up, and we had promptly splurged. I bought a pair of roadside Nike for Wasim, a tricycle for Fatima's son Moin, a gas lighter for Ammi and nothing for the imam. The rest I spent on a facelift.

Nice sunglasses, Imran.
They complete your look of a pickpocket.
– Abbas Chacha (1959-)

Then one day I fished in my pockets and found there was no more money to be spent. Our sortie at Mehendi had lasted a little over a couple of hours, its spoils less than a fortnight. With the city showing no sign of recognizing our talent and bestowing upon us more complex and rewarding assignments, our career options were reduced to a bleak list of bad jobs, the kind of jobs no loving person would recommend to his blood relation: at petrol stations, ice cream kiosks, supermarkets and pizza outlets.

Get a job with Domino's. Uniform is good.
They mightn't even mind those funny sunglasses of yours.
– Fatima Jabbari (1979-)

In spite of our quick and clean operation, the pawnbroker

picked a middle-aged, potbellied gang the next time he wanted a vehicle to be confiscated. We saw them all in the newspaper, stripped to their waists and standing with shy smiles around a table spread with their armaments, most of which looked as outdated as themselves. The pawnbroker stood to the extreme left, looking away from the camera, pretending to be the guy who got these people arrested.

'Next time he calls me, he will regret having dialled my number,' said Navaz Sharif. But when the pawnbroker did not call him even after a month, Navaz Sharif called him to ask if he had any defaulters to settle scores with. No, the pawnbroker said, he had left that business for good. Only big-time criminals and super morons would lend money to the people of Mangobagh. He hung up after a curt thank you, and Navaz Sharif sat staring into the distance like he had more terrible news to share than the disillusionment of an entrepreneur. It was not that nobody wanted our services; it was just that the right people still did not know about us – a lone operation could not have made anyone infamous. We needed something more than a stolen car to be talked about, a bank robbery probably, or a wall with the name of our gang scribbled in blood.

'5½ Loafers,' Zia said in a rare moment of introspection.

'You took the words out of my mouth,' said Jinnah.

In the evenings we played football in the alley where Abu Hathim sahib lived quietly behind heavily buttressed doors, a house from which people rarely came out. When someone fell ill, an old doctor with a weathered attaché case was escorted into the house and back. When the vegetable seller passed through the alley yelling out his wares like a string of abuses, the door of an upstairs balcony would open and a basket would be lowered to the alley on a rope. The vendor sent only the pick of the vegetables up, and knew better than to haggle when the basket descended a second time with some currency anchored with a stone. When death visited the house, the doors opened cautiously for mourners from the extended family and the green casket from Purana Masjid. Not knowing if they would be stopped at the doorway, frisked and then asked to explain their relation with the departed soul, the mohalla-wallahs normally lined the alleyway to pay their last respects. During Ramzan a tiny window attached to the centre of the door would readily open at the ring of the doorbell, and a hand would dole out zakat and disappear before you could admire the many rings on its fingers. You could go twice and get alms without getting caught, but no one dared to cheat, either in deference to the holy month or out of sheer fear of the alms-giver.

The goalposts were imaginary and stood unmanned, but the tackles were real and of a Cameroonian crudeness. The match was paused whenever someone walked down the alley to get to the main street, or the postman rode up with letters for Abu Hathim sahib.

Can't you play your wretched games elsewhere?
Good that Abu Hathim sahib loves football.
Had it been cricket …

– Postman (-)

Abu Hathim sahib's love for football made me love the game even more dearly; I dribbled with a flourish, developed a forced deftness and bore down on defenders with an unnecessary aggression every time I heard Abu Hathim sahib's crutches pick their way to the window through which the sound of a television frequently drifted out. It tickled me to think that Vanity Bagh's hero in exile was watching us, his gaze finally settling on the Messi of the mohalla. Little did I know then that Abu Hathim sahib had long gone half-blind, and could not even see the pigeons perched on the awning below.

The month of Ramzan is here when the pious eat on the sly.

– The madwoman outside the masjid (-2007)

Ramzan turns the business hours of Vanity Bagh's popular eateries upside down. They keep their shutters down till the skies start to darken, and after sunset they do roaring business well past midnight, the smell of spices and meat making pedestrians sniff and sniff as if they are cocaine addicts. Ramzan is a period of relative calm in the mohalla. Siestas get lengthier, swearing less.

As the holy month was drawing to a close in 2007, Vanity Bagh suddenly found itself out of breath and up in arms against its arch rival. Disquiet spread through the mohalla as quickly as the thick aroma of Ramzan-time cooking and nearly, very nearly, plunged the neighbourhood into a full-fledged riot.

Everything was shipshape till the twenty-sixth day of Ramzan. On the afternoon of the twenty-seventh, as the mohalla was getting ready to welcome Lailatul Qadr, the Night of Power, things went topsy-turvy. According to the imam and Ammi, Lailatul Qadr was so special a night that they could not begin to describe it.

> A night holier than a thousand ordinary months,
> when angels descend on earth
> to leave you as sinless as newborns. Do good deeds.
> – Syed Farkudeen Maulavi (1922-2009)

Do good deeds? Even when Mehendi stands in the way of incoming angels? With due respect to you, Syed Farkudeen Maulavi sahib, go fuck yourself. When we get slapped we chop off the hand that has risen to slap us. Angels could wait.

What happened on the twenty-seventh day of Ramzan left the mohalla-wallahs so enraged that they yelled out more invectives in the course of a single day than they must have done in one hundred ordinary months.

Most of Vanity Bagh had congregated in the mosque for the afternoon prayers and was kneeling in the direction of the Kaaba when it happened. We didn't know what had happened in the alley of Abu Hathim sahib's heavily armoured residence until the prayers were over: the screams and shouts from his bungalow were not loud enough to win over the drone of traffic and the hum of prayers. But what we saw was enough to make us want to reach for stones and wield sticks and smash the windshield of every government vehicle that passed through Vanity Bagh, which we did, after listening to eyewitness after eyewitness, one of whom was Ammi. She had gone to Abu Hathim sahib's for her share of zakat soon after we all had left for the mosque.

But you went and took your share last week, Ammi.

This was Wasim's share, Imran. The gentleman is now too big to go and knock on Abu Hathim sahib's door. He thinks it is equal to begging.

She had barely entered the alley when two men passed her on a motorbike. She could not see their faces for their elaborate helmets. This was strange: Mangobagh never cares much about road safety, nor does its traffic department pull up anybody unless they jump red lights. So the only helmeted bikers you find in the city are either anti-social people or people in motorcycle hoardings.

A few blocks from Abu Hathim sahib's house they parked the bike under the neem tree and walked quickly to the tall, riveted door. Ammi stopped in her tracks when one man rapped apologetically on the door while the other fished under his collar for a machete with a beaky end.

You should have shouted for help, Ammi.

I should have, Imran. But my mouth had gone completely dry.

Apparently all eyewitnesses, mostly women, had mouths as dry as deserts and legs that trembled like leaves. On the third knock, the little window on the door was flicked back from inside, and a hand holding a crisp, mandatory ten-rupee note came out. The man who had knocked on the door grabbed the wrist with both his hands and tugged it until the hand was hanging out through the tiny window. His companion raised the machete high in the air, as if he were going to lop off a branch, and brought it down with a yell. Once, twice, thrice ... Some women covered their faces, some others tried to shoo away the attackers, and the rest simply fainted. But Ammi stood perfectly still as the men jumped onto the bike and sped out of the alley.

You should have stoned them down, Wasim's Ammi.

Didn't I tell you my whole body had turned numb, Imran's Abba?

To judge from the timing of the attack, it was a well-plotted attempt to leave Abu Hathim sahib more handicapped than he presently was. They had opted for the afternoon knowing men would be in the mosque; they had chosen the month of Ramzan because it was the only time of the year when Abu Hathim sahib's hand would emerge through the tiny window at a mere knock. But how wrong they were, whoever they were!

Once the wailing, fainting and chest-beating were over, the eyewitnesses saw the door open and Abu Hathim sahib emerge into the alley, both his hands safe by his sides. On that fateful day, probably on all days of the Ramzan month, it was his youngest son Ijaz who had sat with a bundle of currency behind the door and dispensed zakat through the little window. Vanity Bagh heaved a mighty sigh of relief: Abu Hathim sahib was safe and sound, though he was copiously weeping, swearing revenge on those two bikers and those who had sent them.

To the Maqbool Memorial Hospital, where Ijaz had been rushed to, there was a long procession of blood donors from the mohalla; some of the volunteers were even too young or too old to donate blood.

You should also have gone, Imran's Abba.

I don't even have blood enough for my own body, Fatima's Ammi.

I have no clue if it was Abu Hathim sahib who had ordered the ruckus that started by late afternoon, or if it was the mohalla-wallahs who had taken the law into their own hands in undying reverence to their yesteryear hero. The regular rioters grabbed the opportunity and whatever else they could lay their hands on, and hit the street. The enormity of the crime had turned even the celebrated peacemakers of the area into lawbreakers, the most prominent among them the imam, who rolled up his sleeves and ran after a fleeing bus to hurl a fair-sized stone at its windshield.

Don't, motherfucker, don't.

– Commuters (-)

The stone, way off target, whistled its way to the other side of the street where it took off an ancient lampshade that had survived many decades of turbulence and had been the pride of Akbar Electricals. As the flower-shaped lampshade showered petals of pink shards onto the sidewalk, Vanity Bagh, after uncountable years of obscurity, shot into the limelight. All kind-hearted newspapers put us on the front page: medium-sized headlines, fairly big pictures.

Look at your jubbah, Imran's Abba. You always get photographed in your worst clothes.

Next time I will remember to be in my sherwani and fur cap when kafirs come to attack us, Wasim's Ammi.

Not dispirited by the imam's bad dress sense and worse sense of humour, she clipped the picture of him gunning for the bus' windshield (in the picture he still wielded the stone and the antique lampshade still hung prominently outside Akbar Electricals, round and regal) and kept it between the leaves of an old diary.

The buses that ended their day trips at Ashraf Bagh

Terminus had a bunch of late-night visitors, who walked around them with rolls of papers, cans of paint and homemade gum. When the buses resumed their journey in the morning and rattled through the city, people frowned at the posters stuck on their sides and rear windows: BLOODBATH BEGINS NOW. Under the dark prophecy scribbled in the closest shade of blood was the impression of Yahya's hand dipped in red enamel. Beneath the bleeding palm, sketched in green felt pen, the name of our gang made its first public appearance.

5½ Men? Who are these new jokers?
Sounds like clowns escaped from a circus.
– Wasim Jabbari (1988-)

We were particularly harsh on the buses that passed through Mehendi, and stuck the posters even on their windshields. One evening one of those buses came back with a meaner missive pasted over our work of art. LEG FIRST, HAND THEN, HEAD NEXT, it warned. At the top of the poster was a cartoon trident, at the bottom the caricature of a one-legged Abu Hathim sahib. And there started a war of posters which more and more buses from the local depot carried across the city like advertisements for a gangster movie.

On Eid day, dressed predictably in his beige sherwani and black fur cap, the imam seized the microphone by its neck and demanded an immediate ceasefire. Smoothening his sherwani with his palms, he cautioned the gathering that the circulation of any inflammatory material, posters included, did not go well with the spirit of the holy month.

But he relinquished the poise and the topic the moment the congregation was cleaved in the middle to make way for Abu Hathim sahib's wheelchair; he now enlightened us on a less complicated though more jaded topic: how our benevolent deeds in this world would earn us rewards in the Jannatul Firdaus, the after-world. As predictable as his costume for the Eid speech was the final part of his discourse; his voice would gain an emotional twist as he called for brotherhood among the believers, as he assured the gathering how the departed souls would be reunited in the Garden of Allah. A short while later most ofVanity Bagh would hear tears rolling down his voice. Sitting absently on her prayer mat beside her marital bed, Ammi's eyes would well up with tears as the wind carried the imam's tearful voice down the alley, though neither had any idea why the sermon should always have such a weepy wind-up.

I knew you would break down towards the end, Imran's Abba.

I knew you too would weep, Wasim's Ammi.

After the speech, everyone hugged everyone else and the most hugged one, much to the imam's concealed displeasure, was always Abu Hathim sahib, who normally welcomed this spree of embracing with a broad smile. But not this time; propped up on his crutches, he stood stiff and surly as the crowd milled around him and his bodyguards screwed up their eyes to see if the hands that reached out held a knife.

The tiny window of charity remained shut forever after that Ramzan, but news from the house found other crannies to seep out into the alley and spread through the mohalla. Rumour had it that Ijaz Hathim started to wince at the sound of windows shutting and refused to be anywhere near them, even the ones in his second-floor bedroom. The mohalla-wallahs who slept late or very little claimed they heard him wail at small hours, lamenting for his chopped hand, asking the minarets of Masjid-e-Mosavi why his home had become a house of tragedies.

For Vanity Bagh, it proved to be a season of tragedies. One late December evening, Ammi came back from Mogul Bakery with the wisp of a frown on her face.

'Imran,' she gasped, dropping the shopping bags to the floor the way exhausted women do in television commercials, 'Benazir is dead.'

'Oh no!' Wasim, who was lazing on the sofa with his refrigeration manual, sprang to his feet with a sunken face as if it was he, and not I, who had courted Benazir once.

I remembered the Valentine's Day card Benazir had sent me in 2006, a few months before her marriage to the television dealer. She had written 'Forever Yours' in her childish hand next to a pair of infused hearts at the centre of the page. I saw one of those hearts bleeding now, the other all cracked up like broken china.

'What happened?' I asked, trying to sound indifferent.

'I don't know,' she said. 'I just heard people talking in Mogul Bakery.'

'Mogul Bakery is still open?' I could almost see a member of our gang, most probably Jinnah, stepping into the chaotic store to offer condolences and slipping out with something substantial from the till or the racks. 'How is Mir sahib taking it?'

Wasim turned his head to study my profile, where his eyes lingered, as if he were admiring the way Sharif Khan had fashioned my whiskers. The frown on Ammi's face hardened. Then, just as I was beginning to realize my mistake, she spat her words out, 'It is not Mir sahib's daughter Benazir who is dead. It is the other one, Bhutto's daughter.'

The following Thursday, the imam announced the Friday prayers would be lengthier; he would be saying special namaaz for the departed soul. The mohalla-wallahs promptly turned up with tiny black flags of mourning pinned to their chests and the imam, with the help of a hugely erroneous account of her life and times, made the gathering feel enormously distraught about her assassination.

The jumma prayers at the Masjid-e-Mosavi and the imam who led the namaaz found a mention in one of the newspapers the next day.

LITTLE PAKISTAN OFFICIALLY MOURNS
BENAZIR'S DEATH!

And, predictably enough, Ammi cut the news item and kept it between the pages of the old diary, along with the picture of the imam pelting a stone at a blurry brick red bus.

This year you are in the news all the time, Imran's Abba.

Things can only get better from here, Fatima's Ammi.

Before the year ended, there was another death in the mohalla. A death no one condoled and said a special namaaz for. Only a few mohalla-wallahs gathered outside the mosque to watch the men from the corporation wrap the madwoman's body in a mat and load it into a Good Shepherd Society ambulance. Then they drove indifferently towards the last sunset of the year.

VIII

We, the mohalla-wallahs, are patriotic Indians.
But please don't blame Pakistan for every blast.
~ Uncle Ummer Jabbari (1955-   )

Sundays.

I don't like them anymore. It's the day people in a prison, inmates as well officials, fall victim to Obsessive Compulsive Disorder. Those who bathe, bathe for long. Those who whistle, whistle until the wardens signal them to stop. Those who sit alone and smile at their toenails, do that until it is too dark to see their feet. I know how seriously wrong this condition could be. None in my immediate or extended family have this condition. Touchwood, may none in my immediate or extended family ever have it. But Mir sahib's elder brother had OCD (it does sound like a cheap brand of liquor, doesn't it?) and used to file his nails at least a dozen times a day until they found him dead on a toilet seat. But he died of his heart suddenly stop beating, not of running out of nails. According to Mir sahib's eldest son, who refused to enrol for bakery and confectionery training in Switzerland and went to Hyderabad instead to study psychiatry, nobody has ever died of OCD, though every time he was invited by the Rotary Club for a speech he talked about OCD, labelling it an inconsiderate killer.

> No one has ever died of Obsessive Compulsive Disorder.
> But it is a real killer all the same.
> – Dr Shah Navas Mir (1975-)

> Proof that Mir's beta has OCD like his uncle.
> See, he is obsessed with talking about it.
> – Professor Zaheer Ali (1950-)

On Sundays I take especial care to be a normal human being, and do things as different as chalk and cheese just to distract myself. But towards noon I find myself as senselessly obsessive about things as the late Zafarulla Mir. What is bloody wrong with my brain, I ask myself. Why am I humming the same tune over and over again as if it were the only one ever scored? Or doing charcoal sketches of Vanity Bagh on lime-washed walls like the homeless do on the back walls of public comfort stations? Or driving imaginary trucks loaded with silent lambs down roads rolling along green mountains?

These days there is something new I do. I keep wondering what has happened to the piece of news I sent out to the real world through the Workshop man. Is he holding onto it? Or has he spilled the beans? And the NIA is sitting on it because it doesn't trust the source? They surely don't want to dig behind the madrasa and end up finding no bomb. That would be big trouble for the NIA and the government, that would be the lead news on television and bold headlines in newspapers, there would be rallies and riots – and that is my vicious wish list.

Lunch eaten, heartburns burped out, off-duty wardens divide themselves into two groups and play 7s when the sun is behind the line of eucalyptuses. They kick a coffee-coloured ball around as long as there is light in the sky and inmates are there to take sides and clap. This prison loves 7s.

7s was probably the only activity 5½ Men did not have the adequate manpower for. Falling short of one head, we let Jerome Pinto, who had twice kept wickets for his school team, play as our guest goalkeeper. He would turn up in his keeping gloves and spikes and half-sit in the air with his hands outstretched, but his modified skills were hardly tested because nothing ever got past our star stopper-back Zulfikar who, at the first sign of being outwitted by a local Beckham, slipped a hand down the striker's crotch and squeezed his tiny Jabulanis.

What a riot 7s matches were in Mangobagh! The moment they found fourteen people, they set the ball rolling. Under the bridge, behind the bus depot, right in front of the city's biggest garbage hill, even on the little peninsulas frenzied reclamation had given birth to. There were even seasonal tournaments involving big clubs and indoor stadiums, where our place would be only in the stands. We could compete only with our equals: boys from other ill-reputed streets, teams hurriedly made of coolies and vendors from Begum Bazaar, or men from the railway quarters. During an especially hot summer, we were invited to play a team of fishermen in a palm grove near the sea. The invitation came through an exporter of crustaceans who, en route to his office in the fish market, had caught a glimpse of Jinnah balancing the ball on his head longer than it took the lights at the Char Bazaar intersection to change. He pulled over by Akbar Electricals and trudged up to Franklin to praise Jinnah on his extraordinary skills. All great footballers, he said, hailed from the streets. Pretending to be too much of a genius to be moved by roadside eulogies, Jinnah replied he didn't hail from the street but a proper house. All our faces stung with shame. To hide his hurt, the exporter let out a curt, loud laugh. We smiled respectfully and shook hands with him just to make up for Jinnah's complete lack of manners. One thing led to another as the evening traffic flowed past us; he said we looked a promising bunch of footballers, that he would love to watch us play one day.

'Here is my card,' he said holding out a sea blue business card with cartoon fish riding corrugated waves.

'Here is ours,' Navaz Sharif fished out our green-and-white business card from his fake Gucci wallet. (Yes, by that time we had printed business cards for 5½ Men with the line of business specified as interior decorators.) Pocketing our business card, the exporter picked his cautious way through the crawling traffic to his black, lumpy car. We ranked him as the most genuine human being of the year.

Then, when we had completely forgotten about the encounter that he had to repeat the story of the ball sitting on Jinnah's head like a crown, the exporter phoned to ask us politely if we cared to play a team from his village. We said we did. Come fully prepared, he said. We said we would.

The next day we picked seven short-sleeved vests from the Mill Market and got them screen-printed on both sides;

Vanity Bagh United on the chest and the Coca-Cola logo on the back. Coca-Cola didn't even know about our club, so we did not have to seek their permission or sign contracts which would have enslaved us to them for the rest of our lives. But it was a great feeling having the Coca-Cola logo on your back. It was a greater feeling than having a girl on your back.

On a hot afternoon we reached the fishermen's village to an utter lack of welcome. Our host was mysteriously missing. And the man designated by him, an old fisherman who had albino eyelids and orange eyelashes, who was to double up as the referee later in the day, said the host team was still at sea, chasing fish. We sat on the breakwater and screwed up our eyes at the razor-thin horizon like people awaiting dead bodies to wash up on the shore. Late in the afternoon catamarans came ashore with a formidable line-up: coal-dark men with six-pack bodies, whose features were hardened by the sea into permanent scowls. They neither smiled at us nor shook our hands, as if such cordialities would betray their game plan. The referee led us up a short incline into a rambling palm grove. Stripping ourselves down to maroon shorts and screen-printed vests, we huddled together for a giggly oath (the huddle was from cricket, it was Jerome Pinto's idea).

In the middle of the grove was an oval clearing with the sidelines marked in white chalk, which steadily eroded in the breeze from the sea and by the onslaught of fourteen pairs of bare feet. A few minutes into the match, we realized we were playing in the local version of *Escape to Victory*, and Jinnah was finding it hard to keep his ribs away from the elbows of the opposition. And later, just as the wind from the sea was picking up, the fishermen, who had never let themselves lose a match in their backyard, chased us down the darkening groves.

> Machods, never come here again with your bloody cunts.
>
> – Their Captain (-)

> Bhenchods, we can beat you in fishing and fucking too.
>
> – Our Captain (1984-?)

They trailed us with stones and hunks of mud, with a particular vengeance aimed at Yahya who had brought shame to their clan with his stubbly head. Like a whale coming up for air, he had leapt high in the air twice and thumped the ball into the goalpost made of fishing nets. What infuriated the fishermen more than the goals were the theatrics of celebration Yahya had erupted into. They mistook his speech impairment for arrogance, his antics for extreme mockery, and treated him with a volley of missiles as we scampered through borderless plantations.

When the sea fell silent behind us, we paused to get our breath back. It was only then that, leaning against coconut palms and wrapping our hands around our tummies the way Fatima regularly did when she was pregnant with Moin, we realized we were underdressed for the journey home. Marching through the mohalla in our shorts and vests, dripping with brown slush, was unthinkable. Retracing our steps to the clearing to claim our clothes was even more so. The best thing to do was to patiently wait for the mohalla to fall asleep, as patiently as we had waited for the catamarans that afternoon.

Upon remembering that his mobile phone was in his trouser pocket and his trousers were still hanging on the branch of a young coconut tree in the clearing, Jerome Pinto's fingers started shaking like a girl's. We started to laugh at the prospect of George Pinto ringing up his son and one of the six-pack men answering the phone.

Jerome who? Ah, the goalkeeper. He can't talk to you.
His mouth is full for the moment.
– Six-pack (-)

When night fell we found ourselves seated on the sloping walls of a disused canal – seven dark shapes under a full moon, hungry and shamed. Swarms after swarms of mosquitoes barrelled out from the far bank and hummed around us, occasionally knocking against our faces and then trying to flee. We applauded their retreat, catching them between our palms and rubbing them to quick death.

Around midnight we waded across the canal and continued to Vanity Bagh and, crossing the rail lines, walked in the collective shadow of the sleeping mohalla like an army of mercenaries invading an unwary town, which would be surprised out of its wits if it was taken over, and a wee bit proud too for its sudden change in stature – from an infinitesimal dot on the district map to an area under siege.

For a few weeks afterwards Yahya showed off the ruddy swellings on his shoulders, where the fishermen's stones had hit him, like medals; he replayed the two goals in great detail, in slow motion, followed by the cart-wheeling, which was always rendered at a fast-forward pace.

Sundays bring such memories back: some good, some bad but all worth a playback. On Monday mornings I grab a book from my worktable and open it, eager to read from its blank pages, to secretly marvel at row after row of words that draw the map of Vanity Bagh and sketch its people.

In the beginning of 2008, when the mohalla was still so full of sympathy for Benazir that most of the babies born during the period were given the names Bilawal or Benazir, there was the second attempt on Abu Hathim sahib's life – the second in three months, that is.

There were fewer eyewitnesses this time and, unlike the last time, little damage. But the novelty of the attempt was talked widely about in the mohalla and even secretly awed at. There were rumours that Noor Jahan sahiba yelled so loudly and musically that the ladies in the neighbouring houses mistook it for the midday siren from Shiram Glass Factory and chided themselves for being so late with cooking lunch. But they were just rumours; the siren at Shiram Factory had conked many years ago and nobody had ever timed their kitchen chores with its rusty blare.

According to the eyewitnesses, many of whom were actually eyewitnesses to the real eyewitnesses' act of reconstructing the episode, this was what happened that morning. Noor Jahan sahiba was combing her long, silver-streaked hair when a new vegetable vendor entered the alley, singing out the names of the vegetables displayed on the tray of his pushcart. She leaned over one of the upstairs windows and had a quick survey of this new vendor and his wares. From a bird's-eye view, the vegetables looked fresh and the vendor looked an absolute vegetable, and everyone knows how much Noor Jahan sahiba loves to bully morons. She yelled down for half a kilo of tomatoes and lowered the basket into the alley on a rope, hoping to find something even remotely inferior about the merchandise so that she could grill the poor chap. Up came tomatoes, all red and fresh. Impressed, she placed an order for half a kilo of brinjals. Brinjals were sent up, nice and purple. Then she wanted potatoes, a whole kilo of them. Up went potatoes too. The moment the basket reached its destination Noor Jahan sahiba noticed something unusual about a particular potato, which was nearly a perfect orb and had jute strings around it. It weighed like a stone too. Finally an anomaly! She leaned out of the window to probe and found the vendor missing from the alley, though the pushcart was still parked under her window.

Noor Jahan sahiba has a good analytical mind. All those years of living with a don have equipped her with a sixth sense that many women in the locality are completely bereft of. If it had been Ammi she would have happily opened the parcel and got herself all blown up. But Noor Jahan sahiba plucked the strange-looking vegetable from the basket and flung it out of the window, shrieking for God's immediate interference.

Ya Allah Ya Rabi Ya Rahman …
– Noor Jahan sahiba (1951-)

It landed on the pushcart and lay there harmlessly for a few minutes as if considering what to do next before going off with a deafening bang. Cabbages rolled off as far away as the main street. The sound of a mangled pushcart crashing against a wall transcended even the intersection.

Ammi, Ammi, a plane has crashed in our mohalla.
– Aasia Jamal (1992-)

No one thought of rioting this time. When you are on the winning side you don't riot. If you do, you become a loser. But some women came up with the silly idea of wielding brooms and marching down to the post office in protest against atrocities committed against women, as if it were the P&T Department that had sent the bomb up in the vegetable basket. These ladies were just pretending to be feminists or trying to be in Noor Jahan sahiba's good books. Ammi, who is occasionally a genius and frequently a retard when it is time to make her mind up on monumental issues, chose to be the latter this time, readily grabbing a broom and cleaning it up for public demonstration.

For foolish women,
danger lurks at every street corner.
– Our grandma (1926-2001)

Bang on, Grandma. Ammi was striding off with a fake determination to join the small band of broom-bearers who had already congregated outside Abu Hathim sahib's house when she stumbled upon the imam near the paan shop. His face was already set in an expression of utter shock, but that was only natural when you had the misfortune of talking to Jerome Pinto's grandpa.

> Can you do away with your afternoon azan, Jabbari sahib?
> It disturbs my siesta.
> – Jerome Pinto's grandpa (1907-2009)

At the sight of the imam Ammi froze and frowned. It was obvious from the imam's hard stare that he wanted to get physical with her, to kick her so hard that she would fly away like the cow in *Twister* and land on her fours between Tabu and Humera, but Jerome Pinto's grandpa was watching. So the imam rolled his eyes instead, and ground his teeth so hard that his jaw became as taut as Schwarzenegger's. Relinquishing her cause, Ammi turned on her heels and plodded home, dragging the broom behind her like a broken wing. The imam turned around and smiled broadly at Jerome Pinto's grandpa, and suggested he keep his ears plugged.

Nobody we knew could tell us why on earth anyone wanted Abu Hathim sahib dead or maimed. He was no monster, just a retired don. Dons retire, does revenge ever? And dons are always unreasonably hated, that's an occupational hazard. Maybe Abu Hathim sahib in his heyday had eliminated a family by mistake and a surviving son wanted to kill him and make an emotional announcement: 'Mummy-Papa, I killed the killer who killed you. So I am a killer now. Kill me.' Just like in those old movies which reserved the last scene to solve all familial riddles at one go.

After the bomb episode, which gave birth to the term 'aloo bomb' in the lexicon of Mangobagh's detonation experts, the Hathims grew insanely alert and had a Black Box fixed on their front door. There are three steps to use this simple device.

Step 1: Put your face near the Black Box which has an eye at the centre and a hell of a lot of holes beneath the eye.
Step 2: Press the blue button. There is only one button on the device anyway.
Step 3: Soon after you hear a beep, tell the box what is your problem in life. If the Black Box is convinced, one of Abu Hathim sahib's sons or servants will open the door and let you in.

In ones and twos the mohalla-wallahs strolled down the alley to have a look at the Black Box, though they were too frightened to strike up a conversation with it. Only Zulfikar, who had always made us believe that his mother and Abu Hathim sahib were first cousins, had the temerity to have a few words with it. The rest of us stood on either side of the door so that the box could only see him and have a one-to-one chat. He pressed the button, and when it beeped after a minute he said salaam and asked for Salma.

'Which Salma?' the Black Box asked back in an unpleasant voice. 'The one who sews or the one who works in the kitchen?'

Zulfikar blushed. 'The kitchen one.'

'Reason?' the Black Box asked.

'Sorry?'

'Why do you want to see Salma?'

'She is my mother, sir,' he said meekly.

There was a moment of complete silence in the Black Box, followed by the sound of two people talking and goats bleating in the background.

'Zulfi?' a voice breathless with excitement asked.

'Ammi!' exclaimed Zulfikar. He was no longer the man who had wanted to be the leader of our gang a year ago. 'How are you, Ammi?'

Pressed against the wall, we started to titter.

'What do you want?' she snapped. 'What is it that can't wait till I come home in the evening?'

Zulfikar gulped. He had thought the doors would open the moment he asked for Salma Auntie; he had not anticipated questions. He could not even snap back because only God knew who else was listening. 'Abba is sick,' he said finally.

Covering our mouths, we roared with laughter.

'What happened?' the Black Box asked in a concerned voice, which made it even harder for Zulfikar to answer.

'Wheezing?' Salma Auntie asked, much less concernedly than the box.

'Yes, wheezing,' Zulfikar said, shaking his head like a small child.

There was another little period of near silence on the box. All we heard were whispers and the cute laughter of a baby, who Salma Auntie was probably carrying on her hip.

'Zulfi,' she said after a while. 'Take him to Shanti Clinic. The chit is under his pillow. Sohail sahib will give you some money.'

'Wait there,' the Black Box said.

'Sure, Sohail sahib,' Zulfikar said.

The door opened after what could easily have been a quarter of an hour, and that too only wide enough to tightly frame a face. A look of suspicion spread on Sohail sahib's face when he found Zulfikar was not alone in the alley. Quickly shoving two hundred-rupee notes into Zulfikar's waiting hands, he closed the door; we heard latches busily slipping into loops. I counted up to four.

That very week they fixed a camera above the door, which turned its neck like a dinosaur at regular intervals to inspect both ends of the alley. Now even if you stood beside the door and pressed yourself against the wall the Hathims would see you. They might call the police or even unleash on you a pack of Dobermans which they had acquired, much to the imam's displeasure, a fortnight after Noor Jahan sahiba had been bestowed with an aloo bomb.

IX

Can't Hindus make and plant bombs?
Prosecutor sahib, are you accusing Islam of inventing RDX?
~ Corporator Liaquat Ali (1970-)

In theatrical abilities, Ammi and the imam are strange bedfellows. The imam cannot act to save his life while Ammi can make even Tabu and Humera emotional with her dramatics. If she were born in another part of the city, to another set of parents, in another religion, she would easily have made it into soap operas. She would have played lots of mummy roles which don't demand much intelligence, just a lot of tears.

She cried a great deal today, so much so that the young warden, despite his best efforts to appear unruffled, averted his face, wriggling his nose. He is perhaps as young as me but looks much younger than Wasim, and was probably moved by the memory of his own mother, maybe long dead, crying. He now stared demurely at the inmates whose visitors kept their cool and looked fit to discuss a jailbreak. This was the moment Ammi had employed her false tears for. Taking my hands in hers, still weeping, she slipped Big Babols into my hands so deftly that even I didn't realize she had committed a violation of prison rules until she said, 'Don't let them see you chew it.'

I am not planning to chew bubblegum. Why should I? I am not going to kiss a girl outside a dream for the next fourteen years. Nor am I going to appear for an interview in an over-air-conditioned room where bad breath could cost you the job even before you landed it. I am not even going to open my mouth to a lady dentist in the near future. My teeth are fine, thank you. In short, Big Babols are not for me, they are for the cameras. I would just wet them and stick them on the lens when everyone, including the cameras, is looking the other way. At least that is the plan. That's my Freedom Plan for Independence Day, as the telecom advertisements go. Prison has made me a plotter. Prison makes everyone a plotter.

If you walk along the corridors too close to the pillars, the cameras will not see you approaching. Stand behind a pillar pretending to look for something you have dropped and, just when the camera finishes a rotation, reach out and stick the Big Babol on its face. Phut! Repeat this simple manoeuvre six times over and you will have left the surveillance system in the courtyard stone-blind. It is easier to blind cameras with Big Babols than to put dogs to sleep with dried fish dipped in chloroform. I have planned everything in detail. What else are sleepless nights for? In my heart of hearts I want to get Zia out as well. He is a good friend. But it is too dicey; passing on messages is a risk that outweighs even the greatest of friendships. Though I see him playing a part in this daylight jailbreak, he doesn't play an essential part. If I find him on my way out, which is unlikely even on a day when the whole prison gathers in the courtyard, I will drag him along. Otherwise forget it, sir.

Talking of escape, something really funny happened last month. We were in the TV Room, watching the television which is fixed too close to the ceiling that you get a pain in the neck by the time the Sunday movie is over. We should have been watching a movie or a reality show that evening, but it was a news channel that had been forced on us because the wardens wanted to watch an exit poll. The poll findings were being heatedly debated among the wardens when the bulletin turned its focus on an attempted jailbreak in some godforsaken corner of the world. It was as if the lady who read the news could read my mind as well and wanted to furnish me with some good case studies. But this one was of much bigger proportions than I could ever think up or execute. This was a thousand Imran Jabbaris plotting together, not just plotting but acting together. Hell had broken loose in a North American prison. The prison, to begin with, looked like a township, with wide roads, watchtowers, basketball courts, garages and a water fountain. This could be the same prison where they shot *Lock Up*, but definitely not the same cameraman who shot the movie. At first I mistook the inmates, dressed in blue dungarees, for factory workers, and the wardens, in their greyish outfit, for supervisors. After the introductory shots of neat premises and peaceful surroundings, as if it wanted to impact us with a before-after formula, the bulletin treated us with unambiguous scenes of lawlessness.

An inmate was trotting away to a small building with a gas cylinder balanced on his shoulder as if he were an Indane delivery boy. There was an explosion from the building almost the next instant and the roof was on fire. Up what looked like a running track another man in blue was walking a warden at gunpoint; he punched his hostage on the face every time the latter tried to look over his shoulder at the burning roof.

I hope they have already shot
the superintendent through the arse.
– Inmate No. 861 (-)

A gun held to his head, the warden appeared to be working out a deal in whispers; maybe he was volunteering to barter information about secret doors and escape routes for his life. But all his captor was interested in was punching him and punching him like he wanted to set the world record for bashing up a prison official. We all clapped in encouragement though it was not even a live telecast. The superintendent burst into the TV Room from nowhere and quickly changed the channel, and then angrily switched off the television. As if you need a scene from an American prison to start plotting. All you need is six Big Babols, and a little bit of imagination.

Having accomplished her mission with enviable exactitude, Ammi was now drying her face. You could tell from her smile she was very proud of what she had done; she expected a word of appreciation from me. I still pretended to be too grief-stricken to be smiling while my fingers were deftly tucking Big Babols under my waistline. Once done, I asked Ammi not to boast around in the mohalla about how she smuggled in

Big Babols. Unlike the imam, she is a very boastful person. I warned her it would mean trouble for me; what I refrained from telling her was it would be trouble for her as well when I jumped the jail using six Big Babols.

When it was time for her to depart, Ammi was in tears again. But this time she cried for real; her eyes had turned as red as when she chopped a mountain of onions for the Eid feast. The thought of our dark little kitchen with its many smells and silhouettes of urns threatened to plunge me into the depths of despair. I watched her until she reached the spinach beds. Then I walked dreamily across the courtyard where there would be the Independence Day celebrations in a week's time. I put myself in flashback mode.

A week before Independence Day of 2009, the imam brought home something nobody in the mohalla had ever dared to: the national flag. I heard him tell Wasim what he had read in newspapers about the tricolour: the government has relaxed the rules. Now everyone could hoist the national flag wherever they wanted unlike in the old times when only the president, ministers, army people and headmasters were allowed to do that. One rule the government has not changed pertains to the handling of the national flag. You have to be very careful with it: putting it upside down or dropping it to the ground, even by mistake, could land you in jail.

'It's not a new rule,' Wasim said. He was lying on his stomach on the floor between the settee and the chairs, a hand under his chin, hair falling onto his forehead like a little girl's. Directly under his chin was a sheet of pink chart paper, which was eager to roll back to its favourite cylindrical shape but prevented from coiling by four different objects placed on its four corners: a pencil box, a saucer, a clay figurine, an elbow. Wasim was drawing the block diagram of a fridge on the chart paper, which he would roll up and take to the institute in the first week of September. The diagram did not even look like it belonged to a fridge; it looked more like a tiny township seen from a tower crane. You could imagine neat black roads leading to housing estates, arrows pointing to car parks, children's play area, swimming pools and security cabins. I don't know how well Wasim's diagram was appreciated in the September evaluation, but it changed the way I looked at fridges forever. Now when I see a fridge I imagine a housing colony of tiny snowmen beneath its walls; I see the ice tray as a community bathtub, egg racks as pre-historic sites freshly excavated. 'The rule has been there for years, Abba.'

'In my childhood it was a crime to touch the national flag,' the imam said. 'Now you can buy it from every supermarket.'

'You bought this?' Ammi asked, almost incredulously.

'Yes, I bought this,' the imam said. 'And on August 15th I am going to hoist it.'

Wasim looked up from the chart paper, and smiled at the imam as if he wanted to yell, like the cute little girl in the advertisement for cooking oil: *My daddy strongest.* I don't know why, but on that day so many things about him were girlish, school-girlish. Maybe anyone lying on his stomach with chart paper tends to look sissy.

'And where are you planning to hoist it, Imran's Abba?' Ammi asked. 'Inside your room or outside the house?'

'Outside the mosque, Wasim's Ammi.'

Wasim looked up from the chart paper again; he looked prouder of his father than the little girl in the advertisement was of hers, though he was not even ten per cent as cute as her. Ammi pulled a face – she has the kind of face that makes pulling a face the easiest thing on earth. 'Imran's Abba, have you ever seen any flag other than a green one hanging outside a mosque?'

'No,' the imam said defiantly. 'This will be the first time.'

'And the last time,' she said. 'Abu Hathim sahib is only crippled, not dead.'

'Don't worry,' Wasim muttered under his breath, 'he will soon be.'

Ammi wanted to hit him. She at least wanted to tear up the chart paper so his weeklong hard work would be undone in a matter of seconds. But she just gave him a hard stare and went to the kitchen because nobody hits a young man with a hole in his heart or crumbles up his half-yearly project. But there is a limit to the sympathy you can enjoy – even if the hole in your heart is getting bigger in the x-ray sheets – as Wasim was to discover soon.

For the rest of the week, the imam and Ammi argued about the national flag while Wasim, crouched over the pink sheet, added new alleys, parking bays and sewage pipes to the township inside the fridge. There were tiny booths here and there and I told myself these were ATMs, where frosted little men coldly did their banking.

'Mosavi-e-Masjid is not owned by Abu Hathim,' the imam said in the middle of an argument. 'So I don't have to tell him what I do with it.'

'And why should that old man mind if Abba hoists the

national flag outside the masjid?' Wasim asked. 'It's none of his business.'

'If you don't shut up now,' Ammi said, 'that funny little drawing of yours will go straight into the stove.'

That shut Wasim up, but the sudden loss of his lone ally made the imam harden his stand against the hero of Ammi, I and the rest of the mohalla. 'Abu Hathim is just a criminal who has somehow managed to keep himself off police records.'

'And when Hindus wanted to burn all of us alive it was this criminal who saved the mohalla,' Ammi said passionately. 'Where were the mullahs then? Where was your masjid committee hiding?'

I felt a strong urge to rise up and applaud her. But I kept quiet; left alone, Ammi fought her wars admirably well.

'He was not guarding the mohalla,' the imam said. 'He was just trying to save his own family.'

That was the most thankless thing to say. In my childhood I had heard the imam himself narrate how Abu Hathim sahib and his men had patrolled the mohalla like the Border Security Force so no stranger would infiltrate into the republic of Vanity Bagh.

'The entire mohalla is his family,' Ammi said, shaking with anger. And I wanted to say 'Wah' to this, but I held my tongue.

'Maybe,' the imam replied. 'But that should not stop me from hoisting the national flag outside *my* workplace.' This was the first time the imam had referred to the masjid as his workplace, as if he were a clerk of some sort and Allah was his grumpy, fat boss who rarely looked up from his work.

Wasim opened his mouth to say something encouraging

to the imam but then, in the best interests of his drawing, he gulped down his words and started chewing the end of a pencil.

'Kareem Jabbari sahib, you are inviting trouble for you and your family,' Ammi warned, hauling herself up to her feet.

'I'm just trying to make the entire mohalla proud of itself,' the imam said. 'Newspapers might even write about it.'

'Ah,' Ammi exclaimed, sounding almost like Tabu and Humera. 'You just want your picture printed in newspapers again. That's what happens to people once they get mentioned in media.'

The argument, like in the old Coffy Bite commercial, continued over the weekend, in different durations and tempers. Wasim finished the half-yearly project on the eve of Independence Day, staying up late to give ornamental borders to the drawing. The next morning, someone firmly rang the doorbell even before the light under the door could harden to anything significant. Ammi opened the door to Javed Miandad from Minerva Studio. A camera was dangling from his long neck. The sunlight behind him portended premature baldness for him.

'Yes, Javed Miandad,' Ammi asked sleepily. 'You want to meet Imran or Wasim?'

'Neither, auntie,' he said. 'Imam sahib is ready?'

Wasim was asleep on the sofa, his hands tucked between his legs. But I heard his can of deodorant hissing like a pressure cooker in the bedroom. A moment later the imam stepped out into the front room in clothes he usually reserved for days as special as Eid or Muharram. The black fur cap sat on his head like a wig; he had dyed his whiskers to match the fur.

'Are you ready, imam sahib?

'Oh yes. Let's get started.'

'Auntie is also in the frame?' Javed Miandad asked.

'It is not a family photograph,' the imam said slowly, as if the news would break Ammi's heart. 'And you are photographing me in front of the mosque. Not here.'

'Cool,' Javed Miandad said as the imam, suddenly remembering the indispensable accessory for the photo session, rushed in to fetch the national flag. Javed Miandad let me look through the viewfinder at the tender leaves on the neem tree and the hens that pecked around the alley well. 'Don't click, brother,' he kept reminding me. 'It costs money.'

'Where the hell is that flag?' the imam shouted from the bedroom, and Ammi made as if to go inside to help a husband who couldn't track a single thing in the house on his own. But the imam was already in the front room, his face red with anger. 'Where is the flag?'

'Delhi is the national capital of India,' Wasim spoke in his sleep.

'That is news to me, brother,' Javed Miandad said to the sleeping boy.

'Where is my flag?' the imam asked, slapping the armrest of the sofa, sounding like a child.

'I haven't eaten it, Imran's Abba,' Ammi said.

'Where is it then?'

'It was all dirty,' she said.

'So?' he barked.

'I have washed it and hung it on the line.' Her finger pointed to the well, beyond which was the alley's dhobi-yard: three monolithic washing stones and a complex network of clotheslines. The flag lay between two of Wasim's industrial dungarees, still dripping from the late-night laundering. I have no knowledge of what happened next, for Javed Miandad and I fled the scene, offering each other tea from Hussein Chacha's stall.

Jerome Pinto's grandpa saved the day for Ammi by dying in the mid-morning. Ammi insisted we all go as a family and put some nice flowers on Jerome Pinto's grandpa's chest.

'No flowers,' the imam said. 'It's not Islamic.'

'But Pinto sahib was never a Muslim,' Ammi grimaced.

'If you people are going to fight all the way I am not coming with you,' Wasim announced. 'Sorry. You three can go as a family.'

Everyone turned quiet after that. A heart with a hole is the best ever tool invented for emotional blackmailing.

Jerome Pinto's grandpa was all dressed up and ready to go by the time we reached Bethlehem. A nun in white uniform stood in front of a mike and read from a book in a singsong voice; three nuns in coffee brown uniform stood in a line behind her, moving their lips but not really singing with her. There was a big picture of Jesus in the room, as if about to shrug, his hands open. There were four candles in front of the picture. Two were very tall, the third one only half the size of the other two, the fourth a mere stub, on the brink of dissolving into a pool of wax. When the wind from an oscillating fan passed the candles, the flames leaned forward like a family bending its head in prayer. A family of four, just like ours. For a moment I saw Wasim as the tiny candle ready to die out, and I felt sorry for the other three candles that would have to live on in the painful memory of the snuffed-out one.

Javed Miandad took pictures of the important people as they passed Jerome Pinto's grandpa. He refrained from using flash as a mark of respect to the dead man. I tried not to smile when Javed Miandad, standing across the coffin from us, frowned at us through the viewfinder. The imam managed to look devastated as a series of crisp clicks escaped the camera, Wasim looked over his shoulder so as not to feature prominently in the funeral album and Ammi put a finger on a big rose in a wreath as if to take ownership of the red roses the nuns from St Xavier's Cathedral had brought. Just as we were filing past the troupe of one singing nun and three mimicking ones I noticed the Wasim candle go out, wax spreading around its base like tears. Nobody else noticed this little tragedy. I remembered the song everyone except Diana's husband sang when she died in a car crash.

> Candle in the wind. Oh, candle in the wind.
>
> – Queen & Family (-)

Daylight had considerably dimmed since we had gone in to pay our last respects. Just outside Bethlehem, Jerome Pinto was leaning against an old Ambassador with a seriously dented backdoor, smoking and talking to his girlfriend Clara D'Costa on the phone at the same time. When he spotted the imam and Ammi he hid his cigarette and swallowed the smoke but didn't stop talking to Clara D'Costa. I thought his eyes were moist; while smoking and talking to his girlfriend, he must have been crying for his grandpa as well: they were more like friends than grandson and grandpa, knocking down pints after pints of rum when the postman brought the old man his monthly pension. I hugged him tightly and whispered in his ear, 'Sorry about your grandpa, Jerome Pinto.'

Fuck you man, Imran. You are a bloody joker.
– Jerome Pinto (1986-)

I ranked that as the worst behaviour of 2009.

X

My life is my message.
~ Mahatma Gandhi (1869-1948)

It was funny how I interpreted the poster above when I first noticed it on the wall. I took it for an advertisement for some mobile phone service that sold SMS packages to inmates who secretly use mobile phones with secret permission from wardens. Swindlers, politicians, tax evaders, high-class pimps and other well-connected bums live in the network coverage area even when they live in a jail. We, the lesser ones, are the ones who have to depend either on imagination or on telepathy to connect to the world outside the walls. The second time I read the poster I knew it actually was a quote from Mahatma Gandhi, though the last word of the quote still evoked in me the same image as the first time, that of the back of a digital envelope.

I was back to working outdoors, but only for a couple of days. The Book Room, like many other workplaces, was closed till the Independence Day celebrations were over. They needed all available hands to deck up the prison like a big showpiece. In our mohalla, the Pintos resorted to such showoffs to let their church know their Christian identity was intact in a neighbourhood nicknamed Little Pakistan. Everything in Pintos' Garage would have strings of blinking serial bulbs around it, even empty lubricant drums. There would be drummers and buglers, and free red wine and plum cake which they usually ran out of in the first half hour. The main attraction was the life-size stable they built in a corner of the garage on the eve of Christmas. Jerome Pinto's younger sister Mary Pinto always played the Virgin Mary, and the same doll was dusted up every December and handed the role of infant Jesus. Wasim, wearing a wet strip of cotton for a beard and a wise look, once played one of the elderly men from Jerusalem until he abruptly vanished from the tableau. Blue turban, brown staff, white beard, wise look ... all gone between two winks.

Where is imam sahib's son
Antonio Rosario Pintonio Gonorrhea gone?
– Sheikh Zardari (1945-2003)

With a light frown and a half-smile the imam had arrived on the scene a while ago and was sizing up what he would later describe to Ammi as Christmas-time comedy when the tall elderly man towering over the Virgin Mary caught his attention. His frown deepened, smile waned, but Wasim pretended to be a Jerusalem citizen well past seventy, and continued to simper at the flowing traffic. The instant the imam turned his head to shout a question into George Pinto's ear the tableau lost its baby-faced old man.

We later found him sitting on the washing stone near the alley well, the marshmallow-beard in his hands, his left toe doodling tree shapes on the wet earth. 'Please come and bless our home, uncle,' I said passing by. The imam put him on a two-week probation for wearing a white beard, holding a staff and standing by Virgin Mary Pinto while the mohalla-wallahs either strolled by without sparing a second look or stopped by for plum cake and wine. Wasim did not speak to the imam for weeks after the sanctions were lifted, and Ammi ranked them as the worst father and son of the year.

That was in 2004, five whole years before I would be peeled off the mohalla and thrown into jail.

As Independence Day approached, the jail became the same frenzied whirlpool my school had habitually turned into in the second week of August. The superintendent was as unhappy about the preparations as the headmaster. The wardens turned as busy as teachers, and they lorded over the prisoners the same way teachers did over students. Results were much the same in both the places: posters on the walls, streamers strung between trees and secret plans to slip away to the accompaniment of amateurish music on microphones.

I stood in front of the Gandhi poster and watched the inmates wash the courtyard. A thin, broody man strolled around with a bucket of paint, the brush in his hand dripping white, watery lime onto the stones. He paused whenever he spotted a boot mark on the wall and, squatting on the cobbled floor, daubed lime on the blot until there was nothing left of it. Two wardens were walking around with rolls of paper balanced in the crooks of their arms, putting up posters to hide blotches too deep for the paintbrush to mend.

Ignorance is always afraid of change.
– Jawaharlal Nehru (1899-1964)

I liked this poster better than the first one, though I never expected Nehru to be alive as late as 1964. I had always been under the impression that all big leaders died one by one soon after the British had snatched their flags off every single flag post and rushed off to catch the first available plane. But then my understanding of Indian history was pretty bad. Of world history, I had even lesser clue. In short, history was never my cup of tea.

The Independence Day is on August 15.
Unless you are a Pakistani. Then you are right.
It's on August 14.
– Devaki Hegde (1932-1998)

I cried a great deal that evening, copying 'August 15' 250 times on ruled sheets of paper as penance. The night had fallen by the time I had finished, and in the shed at the front of the house a black-and-white goat with a particularly fierce frown had just given birth to Tabu and Humera. The imam was required to sign the document of atonement as if to apologize for the historical blunder his son had committed. But he refused to, and went for a walk in the market; by the time he returned Ammi had forged his signature and even put the seal of the mosque committee on the top sheet to make it look legitimate.

Put him in another school, Bushra.
The same teacher made fun of my son
because his name is Jinnah.
– Jameela Auntie (1949-)

The third poster was bigger than the first two simply because it was trying to hide a bigger patch of naked brickwork than the first two. The man quoted was Abul Kalam Azad, but before I could read what he had to say everyone was looking at me, pausing in their work to smile. I didn't know what was happening until I noticed a spindly shadow beside me on the cobbled floor. I turned to see who was standing behind me, imitating my posture.

Sir, I hope you are happy
with the arrangements.
– Superintendent (10 BC-)

They started laughing, both inmates and wardens. Let them, I thought, I am going to have the last laugh on Independence Day. Then everyone else would be too shocked to laugh, the superintendent would be even too shocked to close his mouth that was certain to fall open at the news of my escape. Once they had recovered enough they would round up Zia and beat the daylights out of him.

Ahhhhhhhhhh …
– Zia-ul-Haq (1984-2012)

He was a good friend, but he turning into a punching bag for no fault of his made me only smile. Hiding the smile in a forced scowl, I put up a show of sweeping the yard as long as the superintendent's shadow was on the cobbled floor. Then I sat down for a quiet dress rehearsal for the August 15 escapade.

I was armed with the simplest of jailbreak kits: six Big Babols and a plot worth patenting. My plan was not to take the beaten path, which led straight to the back wall. The back wall of a jail would always be the first priority of a freedom seeker, especially on an occasion like Independence Day, and I wouldn't be surprised if the jail had a rule which put the back wall under special surveillance on days as special as this. The back wall would not figure even in my wildest dreams. I would use the banyan tree instead. The Book Room affords a view of this sprawling tree which stands a long way off the wall and is thus not plot-friendly. But a branch, probably growing sick of the jail environment, had grown resolutely away from the trunk until it was out of the jail premises by a good half metre. This portion of the twisted bough still looked innocent enough as it was too high to facilitate a safe jump down to the free world, but there were roots descending from it like ropes made of bed-sheets. They did not go all the way down, but they came down reasonably low. You could slide down a dangling root and let yourself go from the end of it and fall on all fours, without even grazing the skin on your knees. I was positive.

A day before Independence Day, as the sun rose gloomily over the Record Room, I woke up feeling like a rocket getting ready for launch – a silent countdown had already begun inside me. I was assigned to tidy up the garden that morning, and I worked as diligently as my acting capabilities allowed, working with hoes and spades and pickaxes so no one would suspect I was mentally rehearsing the jailbreak scheduled for the next afternoon. Zia, unsuspecting and uninterested, went past me pushing a wheelbarrow piled with brick and mortar and broken glass, the strain of singlehandedly navigating the loaded cart lending him the gait of a chimpanzee as he disappeared around the banyan tree to the temporary garbage hill.

Masterji, I want to be
a doctor when I grow up.
– Zia-ul-Haq (1984-2012)

Sure, Zia. Your handwriting is already
like a doctor's. I can't read a thing.
– Shivram Narain (1947-)

Rubbish dumped, the cart empty, Zia came around the tree a while later, wheeling the barrow like a toy but still maintaining the burdened monkey stride. They chose the area behind the banyan tree as the site for garbage because the tree would hide the rubbish from the visiting dignitaries. The tree would hide more than waste tomorrow. I managed a smile when Zia passed me, but he hobbled away without even sparing a glance in my direction. In thirty-six hours he would be the only member of 5½ Men in confinement, but I couldn't help it.

God helps those who help themselves.
– Shair Shoukath (1928-2010)

Mid-morning, a warden signalled at me to stop weeding the garden. I had a visitor. 'My mother?' I asked him. 'No,' he said. 'Unless your mother is a funny-looking man.' I laughed, my penultimate laugh in this prison if my plan worked the only way it should; I would laugh my last laugh from the branch of the banyan tree, then I would take a leap to freedom. I followed the warden across the courtyard, down a series of sunless passages and up a narrow flight of stairs to the Visitors' Room. We emerged into the longish room of red walls as a clock chimed like church bells. On the walls were pictures of local freedom fighters, many of whom, imprisoned for making bonfires out of things made in Britain, had languished in the cells lining the courtyard; a few had even died there. All of them were getting fair treatment today: an inmate with a red bucket and a sponge was moving from picture to picture, mopping dust off the faces of the patriots. In the far corner of the room was the coffee brown jail furniture: rows after rows of benches arranged for the visitors to sit and weep while the visited stared into the distance. The rows of benches, which always remind me of a waiting shed by a tiny boatyard, had no takers today. The lone visitor was standing, looking at his own hands.

Where I had expected the Workshop man or someone from the NIA, there was a lanky youth with a three-day stubble pretending to be a beard. It took me a few seconds to recognize him; I had never seen him sporting a beard before.

'Wasim, what brings you here?' I asked in an incredulous voice as if he had some other business to be in the Visitors' Room than I, Imran Jabbari, his only brother.

He would not let our eyes meet; he could not even decide if it was appropriate to smile in a prison. In the end he merely put a hand to his chest as if to greet me the way one mohalla-wallah is supposed to greet another. Then, frowning faintly at my mud-stained hands, he mumbled, as if someone had forced him to utter those words, 'My heart surgery is scheduled for Thursday.'

We had grown up without hugging each other, we never even fell into each other's arms after the Eid prayers when you engaged every Muslim you bumped into in a bear hug; our acts of intimacy were restricted to handshakes which Ammi insisted we do after our school-day fights. As he stood there with a palm placed over his heart, which had a hole that seemed to grow at the same pace as he did, all I wanted to do was hug him tightly and give him a comforting pat, and say the kind of reassuring words only people on television serials can bring themselves to say on the face of a life-risking surgery.

Wasim's dream to become India's next Milkha Singh was shattered in the year Con Air started playing in Kemps. (It played four shows a day for two months, one show at noon for three months.)

Nice work, Poe. Truly nice work.
– Cyrus the Virus (-)

This boy has a future in athletics. All he needs is
rigorous training and lots of vitamins.
– Coach Williams (1964-)

Coach Williams gave Wasim rigorous training. Ammi filled him with lots of vitamins courtesy Tabu, Humera and a flock of nameless hens. But he collapsed in the classroom after a warm-up session around a tree, crushing the water bottle of another boy and the dreams of his coach and the imam. His nostrils turned red though no blood came out. The coach, the music teacher and I took him to Shahbaz Memorial Hospital in an auto rickshaw that crawled through mid-morning traffic. Everyone was tense, but only I cried. The imam soon joined us at the physician's room where the curtains, bed-sheets and pillow slips were the same shade of green.

> You can postpone and postpone the surgery
> until you can't postpone it anymore.
> – Dr Ubaidulla (1937-2006)

So Wasim had reached the stage where the surgery could not be postponed anymore. I gave him a pat. He smiled weakly with the corners of his mouth. When he sat down on the edge of a bench and stared at the olive floor, where the sunlight turned it glass-like, I noticed his shoes – the Nike I had picked up for him from Fauji Bazaar long ago. My anguish deepened as I pictured the tick-marked pair sitting under his narrow bed awaiting his return from the hospital, slowly gathering dust, turning into a den for cockroaches, cobwebs covering them like faded and frayed shoelaces, until Fatima's son would decide to dig them out, dust them and march on to puberty in duplicate Nike.

In this room of red walls and coffee brown furniture, conversation is always difficult. It was more difficult between two brothers with equally uncertain futures. He mumbled something and I mumbled something back as the man with the red bucket daubed at the freedom fighters' sepia faces.

Then, to my great relief, the warden signalled the time was up. Only in movies does a warden use unkind words to snap the tie between the cruel real world and the unreal prison world.

'See you,' I said as Wasim rose slowly from the bench.

He walked unhurriedly away from my sight, without promising to see me again.

XI

On the day of the blast, Imran Jabbari
was with me the whole day.
Where? Wherever he claimed to be.
~ Haji Masood (1929-)

The sandy mud from the garden stuck to my fingers like hardened glue. It would not go away no matter how hard I rubbed my hands. Equally gluey was the image of Wasim trudging along the flowering bushes and disappearing around the Record Room. I kept seeing him walking past the conical portion of the Record Room that jutted out of a neat alignment of nondescript prison architecture. After Wasim had slid out of view and there was only an empty, steaming road running to a copper-coloured wall to watch, I picked my weary way back to the garden, the sound of the warden's boots trailing behind me like the reminders of Wasim's fake Nike. I kept seeing dust gathering on his shoes, cockroaches slipping in and out of them as they pleased, even a little mouse nosing one of its curled toes. Details so stark that I could not even pretend to weed.

The sun set behind the barbed wires, the moon rose above D-Block and I felt like penning a poem, taking after the most talented and yet the most criticized poet of the mohalla.

If there is a heaven on earth,
it is Vanity Bagh, it is Vanity Bagh, it is Vanity Bagh.
– Shair Shoukath (1928-2010)

Don't copy somebody else's poem
and recite it as your own. At least not when I'm on the dais.
– Professor Suleiman Ilahi (1949-)

Calm down and sit down, please. Else I will disperse the meeting.
Okay, meeting dispersed.
– Rustom sahib (1951-)

Poetry eluded me, as did sleep. I still saw Wasim on his way out of the jail, composing in his head careful descriptions of a place the imam had never cared to visit. I saw him disappear around the red building again and again as in a short video footage looped to run forever. It was an effort to see anything else, but I managed to see myself perched on the branch of the banyan tree, on the brink of descending into a world without walls and wardens. But something held me back, something that made jumping a prison such a bad move even in imagination. I lingered on the branch, hands wrapped around a knotty root, ready to go down and camouflage myself amongst people, until I realized what held me back: Wasim. He should not have paid me a visit. Just by standing there in the deserted Visitors' Room, a hand placed on his heart, he had become an abettor, a wily ally at least in the eyes of the superintendent and the wardens. He would be credited with bringing me the Big Babols and the idea of a jailbreak. They would drag him out of Vanity Bagh, round him up the way I had imagined they rounded up Zia; they would beat him up with the same indulgence and cudgels with which I had imagined them beat the daylights out of Zia.

Ahhhhhhhhhhh ...
– Wasim Jabbari (1990-)

I remembered Chuck Norris in one of those dust-coloured movies, he and his men on the verge of swooping down on a Vietnamese village and spraying bullets with the same glee with which Mehendi sprayed colours on every passer-by during Holi. I remembered Chuck Norris noticing something suspicious at the last moment. He and Sylvester Stallone are always faced with some eleventh-hour complexity, especially when they fight Vietnamese or Muslims.

Operation aborted.
– Chuck Norris (1940-)

Copy that.
– Imran Jabbari (1985-)

I decided not to jump jail. At least till time erased the possibility of Wasim being a suspect. Why the hurry? I would have my chances in October, when there would be another celebration in the courtyard to mark Gandhi's birthday; there would be posters on walls, streamers strung between pillars, speakers tethered to gooseberry trees, inmates singing through microphones – celebrations on a big scale, though not in the same measure as what was planned for Independence Day. As if to seal the deal, I started to chew Big Babol. One after the other until all six were finished and my breath smelled more strawberry than a bottle of strawberry pudding concentrate.

Zia would have company. At least till Gandhi celebrated another of his birthdays in absentia.

You won't be alone, my child.
I'm with you. And I'm in love.
– Shair Shoukath (1928-2010)

We ranked Zia's love affair as both the worst tragedy and the best comedy of 2008. In the annals of 5½ Men, it was the only incident that made tears well up in some eyes from too much laughing and some other eyes because of too much pain.

Zia had hidden his love story from us for what could be a few months or many years. But in the end, as in every tale of romance, the cat was out.

Aasia Jamal?
Aasia Jamal of all people?
– Navaz Sharif (1985-2009)

We looked at Zia in disbelief, wordlessly demanding to share his feelings for this plump girl with funny spectacles with us, or at least to confirm the news. Zia said nothing, he didn't even say yes or no. Leaning against the dark stairway, he stared into the distance.

> Do nothing, lover.
> Just stand there and stare into the distance.
> – Shair Shoukath (1928-2010)

> The meeting is dispersed. No more reciting, please.
> And don't use the mike.
> – Rustom sahib (1951-)

> Ask them to cut the mike, Rustom.
> Because he will never cut the crap.
> – Professor Suleiman Ilahi (1949-)

The stairway still smelled of the rain that had fallen a couple of days ago, the stairs were still clammy and the coldness of the stone seeped in through the seat of my jeans and worked its way down my thighs like a slow wetness, as if I had wet my pants at the news of Zia's tryst with Aasia Jamal. Across the road a tiny, pellet-shaped green light jumped from bulb to bulb along the rim of Akbar Electricals signage. I always think this would be how amoeba would look if it were visible to the naked eye: green, luminous and eternally darting.

'You know what kind of person Jamal sahib is,' Zulfikar said in a lowered voice.

Jamal sahib was the kind of person the mohalla could not accurately brand as anything: he could be a philanthropist or plain eccentric. In the evenings he carried a scoop of peanuts to the roof of the mosque and shared it with the pigeons; in the mornings he handed a 100-rupee note to the beggar under Franklin who, as if by a previously arrived at agreement, handed back ninety-five rupees from his cashbox. He always wore – even to the Water Authority office where he worked as an overseer – T-shirts printed with the logos of foreign soccer clubs at the front and the names of international players at the back. One day this bald, stocky man would be Nistelrooy, another day Messi, yet another day someone else whose name sounded like the sound of a supressed fart. The most contradictory shirt he ever wore was a red one with the name of Cristiano Ronaldo, the most befitting piece from his wardrobe was a canary one with the name of the other Ronaldo. He watched TV with the volume turned up to maximum, beat up his wife every second Saturday and took his family to watch movies every second Sunday.

'Why do you want to marry into a family of madcaps?' Jinnah whispered.

We had been talking in whispers, though there was absolutely no need to. After the evening prayers the imam had padlocked the mosque and hauled himself home after glaring at the glowing cigarette tips on the stairway.

'Anybody else knows about the affair?' I asked.

'Yes,' said Zia. 'Aasia Jamal does.' When nobody laughed at his joke, he stopped staring into the distance and started mumbling the finer details of his private little *Titanic* in the making. 'Nobody else knows. Nobody will know until we are ready to start a life together. She can make her parents put her marriage on hold for two years.'

With a few curled fingers, Yahya asked how she would make her parents wait.

'Higher studies,' Zia said feebly.

'Attending embroidery class is no higher studies,' said Navaz Sharif.

'She will wait,' announced Zia determinedly.

Our Aasia is getting married.
The boy deals in dry fruits. Wholesale.
– Rukhia Jamal (1967–)

She had come to buy eggs from Ammi and was still hanging around after a dozen eggs had been closely scrutinized and put away in her wire basket. Even after Ammi opened her eyes wide in fake excitement and showered sham congratulations on her and Aasia in absentia, she showed no sign of leaving. So Ammi asked reluctantly after the boy, and Rukhia Jamal readily furnished her with the specifics of Aasia's suitor, her sleepy eyes never leaving me as she divulged all vital information barring the name and the address of the groom.

'But isn't Aasia too young for marriage?' asked the cynic in Ammi. She never liked the cynic in Rukhia Jamal, who once wondered – not completely without reason – if Fatima's husband bore a close resemblance to Johnny Lever.

'She is eighteen-and-a-half,' Rukhia Jamal said brusquely. 'Right age for marriage. Anyway, this mohalla is not the right place for young girls to grow up in.'

'She is only sixteen,' I cut in. 'She was born in 1992, no?'

Two ladies with almost identical bloated frames were staring at me: the egg-seller livid with shame, the egg-buyer red with anger. Two ladies, two points of view, neither in favour of me. I tried to read their minds. From Ammi's point of view, I was merely trying to reconfirm a nutty girl's date of birth when I should have looked offended by her rival's statement about the mohalla being a bad place for young girls. From her rival's point of view, I was the one who had corrupted her sixteen-year-old with chits scribbled with statements of love and roses stolen from Mary Pinto's flower shop. How would I tell them I was obsessed with dates, that I had a photographic memory of the imam's rexine-bound ledger, that I loved memorizing digits that, when fenced by brackets and partitioned by a hyphen, became studies in longevity.

When Rukhia Jamal stormed out of the alley with eggs, Ammi declared that the boy who was going to have Aasia Jamal's hand in marriage existed only in her mother's head.

'How do you know?' I asked sheepishly.

'Rukhia bought fifteen eggs from me only two days ago.'

'So?' I was confused. What do eggs have to do with Aasia Jamal's matrimony?

'She just used eggs as an excuse to come here and dream aloud about her daughter's wedding. They can never afford a dry fruits wholesaler. A street vendor would have been an easier to believe lie.'

'You are a genius, Ammi.'

'Yes, I am. And I will throw you out if you continue to romance Aasia Jamal.'

When I made the mistake of telling the gang about Rukhia Jamal's visit, Zia refused to buy Ammi's eggs-as-excuse theory. He threw away his cigarette and sprang to his feet. 'They are having people over,' he said desperately, not bothering to lower his voice. 'They are marrying that poor girl off in a hurry.'

The windows of the mosque were closed, even the louvres, except for a few which were open, and I caught a glimpse of the imam standing by the window nearest the stairway, his head cocked at a difficult angle to eavesdrop on us.

'Look, Zia, you should let Aasia's father decide about her wedding,' I said so loudly that not just the imam but even the pigeons, whom Jamal sahib fed peanuts in the evenings, heard me. 'Parents know what is best for their children.'

Zia called me the son of a rotten, pus-infected prick and the imam, taking the invective too personally, strode angrily out of sight. But he returned a short while later to throw the windows open and, standing under a sooty fanlight with his back turned to an ochre wall, started fiddling with his mobile phone.

'Hello, police station? Inspector speaking? I was complaining to you ...' He talked loud enough for us to hear, he was almost shouting, so we knew he was faking the call – no one in the right frame of mind would dare shout at a policeman who enjoyed the luxury of a caller-ID phone. Almost at the same instant, there appeared a glow in Zia's shirt pocket and his phone started to rattle like a box of broken bangles. Making a face at the blinking green dial, he turned his back to us and took the call. He was now facing the imam who, looking somewhat like an award-winning photograph with light in the background and darkness in the foreground, was still on the phone, pretending to demand immediate intervention of the law-and-order machinery. For a brief moment it looked like the imam and

Zia, standing a few metres apart, were talking to each other over the phone.

Zia shook his head and let out angry grunts at regular intervals while the imam briefed an imaginary policeman about the chaos on the stairwell. And then, almost at the same instant, they hung up.

'They are coming for you with handcuffs,' the imam yelled into the darkness. 'Please don't go away.'

'The poor girl is under house arrest,' Zia said. 'I'm going to have a word with her father. Come with me.'

Zulfikar counted himself out of the delegation; he said Jamal sahib and his father were first cousins, which made him and Aasia Jamal second cousins. Blood relation was his stock excuse to get out of situations. Zia looked expectantly at Navaz Sharif, who had a genuine reason not to come along: Jamal sahib and his father were not first cousins, they were worst enemies. Zia discouraged an enthusiastic Jinnah from being anywhere near his future wife's house, the windows of which Jinnah had threatened to smash when Jamal sahib refused to contribute to Saddam Hussein Peace Foundation, a charity organization Jinnah solely managed and was the sole beneficiary of.

Zia's mobile phone rang a second time as he lit a new cigarette with the stub of the one he had smoked almost to the company logo. But this time it was a shorter call, which ended without Zia mouthing a single word, not even grunting a single grunt. He climbed down the stairs hurriedly and walked towards Jamal sahib's, forlorn and all alone. Out of sympathy for him, I decided to accompany him. Out of sympathy for me, Yahya decided to accompany the two of us.

Aasia Jamal lived in a poky lane which was accessed through an arched entrance sandwiched between two meat shops – Buhari's and Karachi Meat. The shops were closed for the day, and harpoons hung from awnings on nylon ropes like inverted question marks. For a moment I saw our bodies dangling from the hooks like what befell people who dared the Taliban.

At the entrance, Zia paused to take a long drag from his cigarette. He threw away the butt and fished out a couple of bubblegum from his pocket. One he chewed himself, the other I shared with Yahya.

'Have you watched a movie called *Daryl*?' Zia asked, completely out of context, and I sensed he, in spite of putting up a brave front, was as tense about entering Jamal sahib's den as I. He probably now saw what I had seen a while ago – bodies dangling from metal hooks, dripping with blood and urine. The movie talk was his tactic to distract himself, to dispel the fear of being denied entry into Aasia's home, or being kicked out of it as soon as he asked her hand in marriage.

'No,' I said. 'Good movie?'

'Excellent movie,' he said. 'It is about a boy with double brains. He flies a plane and finally sticks bubblegum on a surveillance camera so that nobody can see what he does.' He spat out the bubblegum into the gutter and wiped his mouth with the back of his hand. 'Come, let's meet Jamal sahib.'

(Later that year I watched *Daryl* on DVD. It was first released in 1985, the year I was born. It ran at Kemps in 1992, years before I saw my first English movie. And finally, when I had a chance to watch it, I ranked it as the most difficult-to-understand English movie I watched in 2008.)

At the top of Jamal sahib's door was a gold-plated panel etched with a surah. At the centre of the door was a big peephole that looked like an eyeball. Yahya pressed the doorbell, and the girl under house arrest answered it with a ruddy nose and bleary eyes. A sudden urge to take her in my arms and plant a comforting kiss in her hair parting was swelling inside me when her mother arrived on the scene and glared murderously at her until Aasia Jamal disappeared behind a curtain.

A live soccer match was in progress on a flat television which looked gummed onto the wall. Jamal sahib was watching it from a tattered sofa, dressed in a red football jersey and white bermuda shorts. 'Come,' he said. 'I was waiting for you.' That was a very positive sign; Aasia must have melted her father's heart with litres of tears. The stadium was humming with an anthem while snow fell like popcorn onto the field. Whenever there was a close-up shot of the spectators, these decent-looking people wrapped in warm clothes behaved just like street urchins in rags, waving at the camera and turning hysterical with joy.

'You all love football?' Jamal sahib asked, motioning at us to be seated.

We all shook our heads meekly, sitting down on a sofa more tattered than the one Jamal sahib was occupying.

'Which of you loves football plus my daughter?' he asked without malice, but he was not smiling either. By sliding to the edge of the sofa, Zia identified himself as Aasia's Romeo. Jamal sahib nodded appreciatively at him.

When the singing was replaced by the resonant blare of some strange wind instrument, the stadium sounded like a sawmill, filling the room with the constant whiz of iron teeth cutting through soft wood; Jamal sahib made a face at the television and got up to get the remote from a windowsill, and we saw he was Rooney today. He muted the match and sat down on the sofa, his left heel placed on his right knee.

'Who do you think will win today?' he asked. I was not sure whether he meant which team or which sofa in the room. Zia blushed.

'England,' I said.

'The match is between Manchester United and Manchester City.'

I blushed.

Behind a curtain, Rukhia Jamal cleared her throat and, taking the cue, her husband got abruptly down to business. 'So you are the one who wants to marry my daughter?'

Zia said neither yes nor no; he looked briefly at the screen where the referee blew a muted whistle and sliced the air with a stiff hand. Rooney was lying still on the ground as if he were hit by a missile, then he clutched a shin and started rolling from side to side in immense fake pain.

'I have no problem with that,' Jamal sahib said. But he said it in a tone which suggested he was the only one who had no problem with Zia marrying his daughter. As if in confirmation, the mother of the girl coughed behind the curtain, coughs as unreal as Rooney's agony, who was now limping past the referee, then sprinting like he was late for office.

'You talk to my elder brother who has the final say in all our family matters.'

We never knew Jamal sahib had an elder brother; we never imagined he could have any relation other than his wife, daughter and son Iskander who had died long ago from consuming too much fake cocaine. For a moment I wondered if he was referring to the beggar under Franklin as his elder brother – it could be a joke, it could be the harsh reality.

'I can't talk to my brother because we are not on speaking terms anymore,' he went on, looking absently at the television. 'He thinks I am good for nothing. He thinks I let my son run wild which finally killed him. And he says he will take all important decisions for my family and I just have to obey. My wife reports to his wife every week.'

'No problem,' Zia said enthusiastically. 'I will talk to him in the morning.'

'You can tell him you and I already had a chat about this.'

'Yes, I will do that,' Zia said, consulting his watch to hide his joy and relief. 'Can I take my Ammi with me?'

'That is up to you,' Jamal sahib waved a hand in the air. 'He lives in the alley behind the Irani Café. Fifth house on the left.'

A cold shiver ran up my spine while Zia continued to simper gratefully at the potbellied Rooney. My mental GPS worked better than his. I stared at Yahya, who smiled and shook his head happily, ready to shake Jamal sahib's hand and then press the shaken hand to his heart.

You might know my brother.
His name is Abu Hathim.
– Jamal Hathim (1962-   )

The three of us sprang to our feet together as if we had become conjoined since we had been ushered into the house.

Jamal sahib picked up the remote and restored the hoots, horns and carol-like singing in the stadium to the room as we marched towards the door. Then he changed the channel.

> Kalawati's husband committed suicide ...
>
> – Rahul Gandhi (1970-)

'So?' Jamal sahib asked the TV irately as we filed out of the house.

Three months later, a thirty-one-year-old dry fruit dealer married the sixteen-year-old Aasia Jamal. He was not a wholesaler, though. That was some consolation for Zia and my Ammi.

XII

By the time we reached his home,
Accused No. 4 was already dead.
~ Inspector Machangada (–)

I touched Will Smith yesterday. That is to say, I touched something that had been touched by him a few years ago. That is to say, I shook hands with someone who had shaken hands with him in 2009. When you have physical contact with famous people, their fingerprints don't wear off you, they get passed on like viral fever.

Welcome the king of sound engineering
who won the Oscar for the best sound.
– Dy Superintendent (-)

The king of sound engineering raised a hand and waved at us the way politicians do; for the last twenty minutes or so he had been smiling the smile of a spiritual leader: the fake, nonstop smile. On the table before him was what Will Smith had handed him with a handshake, a smile and half a hug: the golden figurine that looked like a Phantom statuette with the wrong choice of colour. Could this be the real one? Or was this just a replica? If they part with it every year, it could be gold-plated. If they don't, it is definitely twenty-four-carat. The Muneer Shah Memorial Trophy, which is real gold plus six real diamonds, belongs to the winning team only as long as the photo sessions last. After the press drives away, the victorious club goes home with a replica that is golden only in colour and the six equidistant objects around the base of the trophy are glass pieces pretending to be diamonds. But the Oscar is not the Muneer Shah Memorial Trophy. The first never leaves your mind, the latter never leaves Muneer Shah Trust.

When his turn came to address the inmates, the king of sound engineering made a mess of his speech. He started by saying he was happy to see us all. But then he changed his stance and said he was saddened to see precious human life wasted in captivity. That he would be happy when we roamed the world as freely as the rest of humanity did. Then again, probably fearing he was instigating mass jailbreak, he said we should make the best use of prison life to cleanse our conscience and make ourselves better human beings. Then he contradicted himself by saying that every human being in the world was good and golden at heart. I think this was his real extempore speech and not the one, as he claimed, he had delivered at the Kodak Theatre with Will Smith smiling sympathetically by his side. We all applauded him nevertheless.

You know the difference between you and me?
I make this look good.
– Will Smith (1968-)

Misinterpreting our frenzied clapping for an act of sarcasm and pretending that he was not ruffled by it, the king of sound engineering waved at us and sat down, but the superintendent leaned sideways to whisper something in his ear which made him stand up again. With an apologetic smile he declared the Independence Day celebrations open. We applauded him again.

Autograph hunters,
line up on the left side of the stage.
– Dy Superintendent (-)

The whole prison lined up and a warden distributed scraps of paper – I recognized these scraps: they came from the piles of waste from the Book Room – as the queue crawled up a temporary flight of stairs leaned against the side of the stage. The August sun beat down on us, and enthusiastic autograph hunters started to bicker. Some swore at the superintendent's mother, some at the chief guest's father. The king's smile was still untired when the turn for the man in front of me came, his signature still as lengthy as his name in spite of having been repeated more than a hundred times already. This man probably knew glory came stamped with a date of expiry, he probably doubted if it would ever come his way again.

Now we were face to face, I on the sunny side of the stage and he, the man who was half-hugged by Will Smith, on the shady half of it. He waited patiently with the superintendent's pen while I, to everybody's surprise, ran a hand over the statuette on the table. The king's smile brightened by many degrees, the superintendent's smile dimmed by many more.

'Is this the real one or the replica?' I found myself asking.

The king still smiled, not very pleasantly though. The superintendent looked as if his stomach was suddenly upset; he turned his head sharply to look agitatedly at his deputy, who turned his to look agitatedly at me. The king quickly doodled on the scrap of paper I held out, he hurriedly shook the hand I thrust at him. 'I love Will Smith,' I told the king as the deputy superintendent signalled me to move on with the scrap of paper scrawled with a signature sound engineering had made worth standing in a long queue for.

Across seven seas from the Kodak Theatre, the Oscars of 2009 made Vanity Bagh cross swords with Mehendi. It all started with a poster pasted on the back of a bus, but it didn't stop when the bus was mobbed near the Air India building and set on fire. The poster was in green felt pen, signed with the impression of a hand dripping red emulsion. It stated nothing but the obvious: OSCAR SCORE. MUSLIMS: 3. HINDUS: 0.

We knew the bus was doomed the moment it left the depot happily tootling. What surprised us was the amount of time it took for the poster to be read and reacted upon. The bus had plied through the heart of Mehendi twice in broad daylight without anybody caring to read the Oscar special communiqué. It would have made the third round too had it not been for a teenager who happened to be trailing the bus on his bike. He called his uncle who was the treasurer of Mehendi Hind Sangh; the treasurer called the secretary, the secretary called the president, who called everyone and they set the bus on fire.

We would have been heartbroken if the bus had ended the day's trip with the poster still intact on its arse.

No pain is bigger than the pain you feel
when your words come back unread.
– Shair Shoukath (1928-2010)

You finally admit you are
an unpublished poet? Good.
– Professor Suleiman Ilahi (1949-)

Shoukath miyan, put the flower vase down.
Poetry Club was not formed to promote martial arts.
– Rustom sahib (1951-)

The commissioner of police termed the act of torching the bus as an act of overreacting to a rumour.

'Rumour?' the press asked him. 'There was a poster, no?'

The commissioner was known for his short temper, especially when he sat in a pool of white light and confronted more mikes than he could count. 'Then where the hell is that damn poster?' he asked the press back. 'You haven't seen it. I haven't seen it. 99.9 per cent of Mangobagh hasn't seen it.'

Only a crowd of less than fifty people claimed to have read it, and they were the same people who had made the bus look like it had been driving through hellfire.

'Then what caused the arson?'

'Probe is on. We are actually interrogating the transport company officials. We don't know if the bus was torched by the owners to claim the insurance money. The matter is put to rest till we have the forensic report.'

Only if it was. Even before the Oscars physically reached India and were taken on a victory lap around the country, there appeared another scorecard which was stuck on the windshield of Abu Hathim sahib's youngest son's car.

The Post-it note read: *Muslims: 1. Hindus: 0.*

The car was parked near a gambler's den on Broadway Street, and Rasool Hathim sat behind the wheel, clutching the gear shaft, strangled with a deep orange – almost saffron – ribbon.

'Is this a sequel to the bus burning episode?' the press asked. 'The Post-it note too had a score, no? Just like the poster.'

'There was no poster, to begin with,' the commissioner said. 'And this is a sequel to nothing.'

'What is the motive then?'

'It either has something to do with the hawala racket or a love triangle. We have separate teams investigating into both possibilities.'

Abu Hathim sahib seemed to be sharing the fate of the man who goes for a jungle combat with a bunch of gun-wielding, bandana-wearing men. No one, except our man, survives the jungle. He survives to bury the dead, settle the scores and then passionately kiss a hay-complexioned lady in a floral frock with his warpaint still on. I don't remember the name of the movie. I never had a head for complicated movie names.

Rasool will be avenged.
– Abu Hathim sahib (1931-)

Inconsolable Ammi was. She recounted how Rasool once

came to her aid when things were coming to a head at Dey's. She had had a fight with the security guard for emptying a mouthful of betel juice into a flowerpot put up for sale. Rasool strolled down an aisle and stood watching the argument for a while. Then he stepped in. When he intervened, there would be no more argument, only the final verdict. He wagged two butter-coloured fingers in front of the bewildered eyes of the liveried man, saying he should never forget to behave in the mohalla, especially with this lady, whom he considered as his elder sister. Ammi was flattered. And the guard, with two sausage-thick fingers placed perilously close to his eyes, promised to behave himself for the rest of his life, though Securitas withdrew its service from Dey's the very next day. This happened a few weeks before Rasool stood in the elections to serve Vanity Bagh in a corporator's capacity. He lost miserably, though, by a margin bigger than the number of frauds in the area.

Overwhelmed by the memories of this brief encounter, Ammi skipped breakfast and lunch. By suppertime the good old memories appeared to have ebbed away, for her appetite had returned, although she was still making faces in the general direction of Mehendi.

'Just wait,' she muttered, shaking a finger at her own shadow. 'Just wait till Abu Hathim sahib is ready for you.'

'I don't know who you have asked to wait,' the imam said. 'But whoever they are, they will die waiting for Abu Hathim to be ready.'

Wasim started chuckling. For some reason, the mohalla was less touched and far less angered by Rasool's death than by other tragedies, many of which much smaller in comparison, that struck Abu Hathim sahib's family as regularly as Salman Khan changed his girlfriend.

'Every member of your masjid committee will die waiting for Abu Hathim sahib to die,' she whined. 'Every single member, I mean.'

'Children born to fighting parents usually turn out to be criminals or cracks,' Wasim warned.

'Your words of wisdom have come a little too late, Wasim miyan,' the imam heaved a dramatic sigh, casting a quick glance at me. 'That has already happened in this house.'

In time everyone forgot about Rasool's murder – the press, the commissioner, his A team investigating the possible involvement of a hawala racket and his B team of Rasool's mistress and her paramour, more or less everyone. I don't know if Abu Hathim sahib still lamented over his son – there was nothing to suggest that he renewed his pledge to wipe out Rasool's killers; when he had first uttered it over his son's body, the fortitude in his voice had made Mehendi's stomach churn and its hair stand on end.

Three months after Rasool's death, the recognition that every single soul in filmdom dreams of winning and thereby qualifying themselves to deliver an extempore speech of gratitude arrived in Mangobagh. Out of the three winners, two had declined the invitation from Mangobagh Movie Masters, better known as 3M, suspecting it to be nothing more than a third-rate club run by crooks, which it actually was. The third one, the king of sound engineering, jumped at the invitation and landed in Mangobagh with the golden statuette, using it to punch the air at the arrival terminal as if he had just won it, not three months ago.

3M had built a stage in a corner of the parade ground: they put the main sponsor's logo on the backdrop and the co-sponsor's logo forestage; they let retailers tie their banners between lampposts, charging them according to the size of their advertisements and the visibility they enjoyed. They even did speech rehearsals for the next evening, using a smiling, bearded man as the dummy of the chief guest. Only then did they go home to catch some sleep. A few hours before a shimmering sun rose above Mangobagh's foggy horizon, the stage went up in flames.

Wrapped around a tree trunk was a poster, a new scorecard. *Hindus: One Muslims: Zero.*

'We have all seen that poster,' said the press. 'So you can't deny it this time.'

'Why should I say there was no poster?' asked the commissioner. 'Have I ever done that?'

'So do you think this has anything to do with torching the bus? The bus had a poster crediting one religion with India's performance at the Oscars, no?'

'No, no, no,' the commissioner blurted out. 'There was no poster on the bus. It had nothing to do with any religion or any Oscar.'

Before he caught the evening flight out of Mangobagh, the king of sound engineering paused at the departure terminal to show a thumbs-up sign to the press, as if he had bagged another Oscar overnight. He said he loved the city, that he sincerely regretted the stage had had a short-circuit issue and the organizers did not have the courtesy to apologize to him before they went into hiding. But this city was fabulous, full of interesting sounds. If he was invited again, he would definitely revisit the city.

Was that why he came back to declare the Independence Day celebrations open? Had the superintendent invited him?

XIII

This boy Imran visited orphanages every week.
With sweets and a sweet smile.
~ Haji Akram Shirazudin (1945-)

Zia escaped on the afternoon of Independence Day.

Late in the evening there was a long blare of the prison siren to herald his freedom. I heard boots trampling down the corridor, jeeps leaving the prison wailing and coming back quietly and thunder rolling in the distance over the city. But only this morning did I realize that it was Zia who had caused the last night's commotion, except the thunder.

It did not surprise me that no one cared to interrogate me; what left me flabbergasted was how Zia copied the idea in my head without my knowledge and implemented it without a flaw. As most of the prison sat on its haunches to watch the king of sound engineering talk and then lined up for his autograph, Zia was clawing his slow way up the banyan tree. While laying claim on the ownership of the plot I have to admit that Zia added his own subplots to make my script watertight. He even chose the right costume and picked the perfect accessories, which made his escape the talk of the town here in the prison and out there in the city.

Zia chose his ensemble backstage, from the rucksack of the carpentry instructor who was in the green room, his pancaked face being fixed with an enormous moustache which transformed him into a diabolic king destined to abduct an inmate cross-dressed as a woman of high morals. Zia disconnected a mobile phone which was hooked into a temporary plug point; this belonged to the make-up man hired to turn skits and tableaux stage-worthy, and was later recovered from a waste bin a few miles from the prison. Then Zia could have chosen from a fairly big collection of wigs, fake moustaches, false whiskers and close-to-real facial hair. But he, rightly, did not; any of those could have made him conspicuous, an easy suspect. The last item he pinched before slipping away from the back of the stage in civilian clothes was a nice pair of sunglasses; nobody knew whom these belonged to. Some swore they belonged to the deputy superintendent, some others claimed they saw them dangling from the V-neck of the burgundy tee the king of sound engineering wore as he was taken on a tour of the jail premises.

Nobody noticed him till he had climbed the tree and crawled halfway down the branch that had overgrown the jail premises. On the other side of the wall was a clutter of old buildings where the archaeology department used to function before it had been shifted to a new complex near the collectorate (I had imagined trees stood in tight clusters on the other side of the wall and a tiny house sat in a corner of the estate). A sweeper dressed in khaki was watching Zia from the shade of the branch he perched on. I would have panicked. But Zia whipped out the make-up man's mobile phone and pretended to dial a number. A phone rang in a fictitious pocket for a long time without being answered. Then Zia struck a pose of humility and briefed an imaginary superior that he did not detect any suspicious activity on the east side of the prison. Halfway through the call, Zia pretended to have noticed the sweeper for the first time and knitted his eyebrows in serious apprehension. He ended the call after informing the imaginary boss that he had spotted a man who might have some information on the fugitive.

Straddling the dangling roots, loosening and tightening his grip alternatively, Zia reached the ground to interrogate the sweeper. The officer asked stern questions, the gentleman fumbled for answers, probably dreading that he would be mistaken for the runaway prisoner and manhandled before he had a chance to produce his voter's ID. The officer asked if he owned a motorcycle, the gentleman said no, only a bicycle, which he was more than happy to lend.

So Zia collected clothes, a mobile phone, a pair of sunglasses and a bicycle en route to the highway of freedom. But a man dressed in clothes two sizes smaller for his frame, sporting sunglasses, wielding a mobile phone, riding a bicycle never entered Vanity Bagh on Independence Day or the days that followed.

We're always fascinated when we
find leg irons with no legs in them.
– Tommy Lee Jones (1945-)

His absence was first noticed at sunset when the sweeper

came to the prison to reclaim his bicycle. At first the sentry refused to let him in, then he was taken to the deputy superintendent and a few minutes later the siren began to wail like a song of praise for Zia, whom the sweeper had described as an Akshay Kumar lookalike. The sweeper either suffered from diminished eyesight or mistook someone long-faced and droopy-eyed for Akshay Kumar. Or Zia probably wore the kind of sunglasses Akshay Kumar always did. None of the things he had decamped with were ever recovered, except the mobile phone, which was handed back to the make-up man after the Cyber Cell investigated the call register. Only two calls were made since the phone had been thieved; the first to the central railway station, to warn about a bomb that had been planted in a moving train. I know where he got the idea of a bomb scare to distract the police – we had watched *Speed* together in Sharif Khan's hair salon. The second call was traced to a cripple living in an alley behind Vanity Bagh's lone Irani Café. The call lasted precisely six minutes.

What I earned from Zia's escape was enlightenment: that you need something more than Big Babols to jump a prison – you need brains and balls; that I will continue to attempt jailbreak, though only in my fantasies.

In spite of thunder rolling in the distance every evening, August passed without rains, without Ammi visiting. I didn't even expect her to, what with Wasim's surgery and the possibility of men in civvies roaming around the mohalla eating peanuts. I looked forward to the rains, inhaling the smell of earth that drifted into the Book Room from the garden. Between binding books, I continued to read from their blank pages and think of the smell of raked earth that always pervaded the alleys of Vanity Bagh before the rains. I saw the rain falling through the branches of Franklin with a patter, drumming on the tin awnings of roadside stalls.

One day I looked up from a book and saw it had started to rain quietly. On the floor of the quadrangle the silent rain had collected into tiny pools, and fingers of water rolled lazily down as the rain thickened, bridging Lilliputian islands. It was September. In September, Mangobagh skies invariably poured.

Bearing the imam's ancient umbrella, Ammi called on me on a rainy Wednesday, bringing two medical bulletins from Shahbaz Memorial Hospital. The first she delivered with a smile framed in a sigh: Wasim was making good progress after the surgery; the second with a heavy scowl bordered with tears: Abu Hathim sahib was dying.

Cowards die many times before their death.
The valiant never taste of death but once.
– Shair Shoukath (1928-2010)

Now you are stealing from Shakespeare.
That's improvement.
– Professor Suleiman Ilahi (1949-)

That's Shakespeare? Sure?
I thought Majrooh Sultanpuri wrote that.
– Rustom sahib (1951-)

After the bad news was lamented over for a few minutes Ammi told me what befell the mohalla on the day Zia escaped from the prison. Like on the last two Independence Days, the imam had made plans to hoist the tricolour in front of the mosque in the morning, and for the third year in a row Ammi deprived him of that proud moment by hiding the flag in her cupboard. The imam, unlike on the previous occasions, refrained from raising his voice; Wasim's surgery was due in a few days. Late in the evening, the mohalla overflowed with khaki. Policemen wandered down alleys, shone torches into cowsheds, stopped strangers, had free refreshment from roadside stalls, demanded identification proof even from beggars and tugged at beards that looked unreal.

My beard is my personal property.
Please ask my permission before touching it.
– Inzamam-ul-Haq (1990-)

Of all four brothers, only Inzamam looked somewhat like Zia, and for some time there was talk of Inzamam being taken into custody.

If looking alike is a crime,
half of China would have been in prison.
– Adv. Fakir Ansari (1957-)

If being related to a criminal is a crime,
show me the arrest warrant for your commissioner's wife.
– Mrs Fakir Ansari (1954-)

(A word to those who share my penchant for dates: Adv. Fakir Ansari's year of birth is not a mistake from my side. He actually married someone elder to him.)

The police threatened to arrest the Ansaris for abuse and disruption of duty, and the couple readily offered their hands to be cuffed, as if they were playing the lead roles in a Maoist street play. But in the end the police went away without even arresting Inzamam, leaving the Ansaris triumphantly shaking each other's hands. The police left Zia's tiny, overcrowded house that overlooked a construction site, but they did not leave the mohalla altogether. A group of them operated incognito, waiting for buses, selling lottery tickets, doing land surveys, hunting for jobs or being plainly pious. In the simple disguise provided by an Islamic cap, one of them sat in a corner of the mosque and spied on the imam, who, under the guise of a fool, repeatedly requested the newcomer to contribute to the Tabligh Conference by his presence and through donations.

Abu Hathim sahib denied having received any call from any runaway prisoner. He no longer had access to the number Zia was said to have dialled from the make-up man's phone; he had misplaced the phone on one of his rare trips to Hyderabad – a good riddance as he longer enjoyed talking, on the phone or one to one.

As the police, impervious to Sohail Hathim's pleas to spare his father on health grounds, continued to ask him the same difficult questions over and over again, Abu Hathim sahib's kidneys abruptly collapsed.

> Abba's kidneys collapsed, Abba's kidneys collapsed.
> Call the police. I mean, call an ambulance.
> – Sohail Hathim (1973-   )

An ambulance, which had been spotted in a different part

of the mohalla for the past three days, finally switched on its beacon light and siren and rushed Abu Hathim sahib to Shahbaz Memorial Hospital where he has been progressively dying ever since.

Then came the NIA. But they came quietly this time, in fewer numbers and in smaller vehicles than when they had come for us. They discreetly led a man in a blue tie around the mosque, along the ablution tank, past the madrasa to the patch of grass under the willow tree.

'A fair guy with lots of gel in his hair?' I asked.

'Yes.' Ammi looked surprised. 'How do you know?'

So the Workshop man had finally spoken up; he must have opened up fearing that Zia had jumped prison just to disinter the crates of detonators from beneath the pot of green dahlias and build a spoor of bombs across the city, one too close to his house or office. It still confused and saddened me that I was not a part of the entourage.

The covertness with which the NIA arrived bore little fruit in the end. A crowd thronged the mosque, slogans rent the air, the police drove up in riot gear, at the sight of which shops downed their shutters. The imam neither pacified the crowd nor provoked it. He just spoke his heart out in a high-pitched voice. In the capacity of the highest official of Masjid-e-Mosavi, he warned the NIA that digging beneath the willows would yield only a heap of bones. A little boy's bones. Bones are fossilized memories. Don't let spades and hoes cut through memories. Don't make minds bleed. The crowd cheered the imam's rhetoric.

Bones are fossilized memories.
– Kareem Jabbari (1953-)

Listening to Ammi's account, I can't accurately say if it was the imam's oratory that influenced the NIA's decision to not dig. Putting the spades and hoes and pickaxes away, they spoke to the people who claimed to have attended Sinbad's funeral, verified the mosque's records and, after waving a couple of bomb-detecting devices around the willow tree, deduced that the pit under the pot of dahlias contained nothing but fossilized memories.

As the police escorted the NIA out to the street, the imam clambered onto the parapet of the madrasa and did a tailpiece to his short yet spectacular speech about bones. Shaking a finger, he said his heart beat for hundreds of thousands of innocent people who were languishing in dark cells without a trial. Wiping a tear, he reminded the dissipating crowd that his own innocent son had been snatched away from him and flung into a sunless chamber.

The last part was the least convincing; I seriously doubted that Ammi had made it up, though she vehemently ranked it as the imam's best speech of 2011.

XIV

Justice delayed is justice denied.
I request you to expedite the proceedings, My Lord.
~ Public Prosecutor (-)

The drawers of my worktable have been opened and ransacked. The yellow feather, the bookmark that fell from the sky, is conspicuous by its absence. I look around in search of it and finally spot it in the hands of a warden, most of its quill already inside his ear. His one eye is closed, and half his face is all wrinkled up and set with the indescribable pleasure of being tickled on the eardrum.

I feel utterly lonely, but the loss of my bookmark has nothing to do with it. I am grieved by bigger losses which are actually too big to be evaluated without help. I remember the lone survivor of the jungle combat team, the glassy-eyed, lantern-jawed soldier who hauls himself towards the last reel of the movie. I feel like him. I don't know what remains of 5½ Men, I don't even know how many of us have survived

11/11. All I know is: I am alive, and I am alone, and I can read from blank pages.

The warden finishes cleaning his ear with the feather, looks up and sees me staring at him. He stares back, jerks his chin questioningly, enquiring with a finger pointed at the feather if I need it to clean my ears. He then sends the feather out of the window by launching it into the air like a paper plane. Had this happened in a jailbreak movie, this would have been reason enough to start a prison revolt.

This is hell, and I'm going to
give you the guided tour.
– Donald Sutherland (1931–)

Your body has to be here.
Your mind can be anywhere.
– Sylvester Stallone (1946–)

I open a book and stare at its pages. I see it raining in the mohalla.

When it rained, the roof of Khan Hair Salon sounded like the audio tracks of *Rambo I*, *II* and *III* played back to back. It was just raindrops tapping on tin sheets, but it sounded just like Stallone slaying Vietnamese revolutionaries in the next street. When it rained the best thing to watch after business hours was porn. Navaz Sharif had the run of the salon from the evening, when his father, tired from standing all day behind salon chairs and eyeing his own reflection in the mirror like a strip teaser, retired to nurse a bottle of cheap liquor.

Never shave a customer's armpits,
even if he offers to pay double. Or even triple.
– Sharif Khan (1950-)

Ironically, Navaz Sharif's work-related fantasy involved shaving a famous Pakistani lady's armpits, that too for free. After bundling off the last customer into the rain-washed street, we reclined on salon chairs and reflected on the crisis pornography was faced with on a global scale, the crisis of cliché, while muted couples made out on a fairly big flat screen. The desi ones were the worst; they would not even look properly at each other, let alone kiss passionately.

....
– Over-conscious lady (-)

....
– Over-emoting man (-)

It was early November and raining. There was talk of truncating power-cut hours or even lifting them altogether as it had been raining steadily in the catchment areas. On the screen a South Indian girl was glaring at her potbellied Sindhi-looking partner for attempting to do something she had not been told about beforehand. It was obvious that she was going to create a scene once the camera was switched off. Her partner was squinting at the camera and restraining a burst of laughter as a shadow, probably that of the man who had funded this home video, darted across the wall behind the narrow bed. Then they were back to the business of frisking each other and perfunctorily kissing.

Navaz Sharif, Zia and I gave the video a single-star rating, Jinnah and Yahya gave it two on ten and Zulfikar opined we should stop ranking and rating every damn thing under the sun, especially porn. We were wondering if we should rank Zulfikar as the top hypocrite of 2009 when someone rapped on the door.

'It's Abba,' Navaz Sharif gasped, quickly wrapping a towel around my neck and starting to trim my hair. Jinnah ran to the rack on the wall and unplugged the DVD player and, to further obliterate signs of debauchery, veiled the TV in a satin cloth. Zia and Zulfikar straddled a bench and started playing chess with serious concentration. The door was knocked more insistently than the roof was thumped by the rain.

'Don't cut my hair,' I told Navaz Sharif concernedly.

'He will kill me if he finds out we watch porn in the shop,' Navaz Sharif said even more concernedly as Yahya opened the door and let the sound of the rain in.

'Checkmate,' Zia said, slapping his thigh.

'Oh shit,' Zulfikar yelled in cooked-up anger. 'You beat me again.'

In the mirror I saw a thickset man standing by Yahya and sizing up the shop with a mild distaste; the air was suddenly redolent of jasmine attar.

'We are closed,' Navaz Sharif told the stranger with an apologetic smile. 'This is my last client of the day.' The pair of scissors snipped menacingly close to my ear.

'Oh, I don't want a haircut,' laughed the stranger, running a hand over his bald head. 'What is there to cut anyway?'

All, except me, turned their heads to look at him. To do justice to my role of a client, I had to content myself with his mirror image. Of course I had seen him before, not once but many times, but whether it was here in the mohalla or elsewhere I could not recollect.

'No, I don't want the services of a barber,' he said, much to the chagrin of Navaz Sharif, who thought 'barber' was the job title for a Hindu, while 'hairstylist' was the cosmopolitan term. 'But I want to hire 5½ Men for something.'

The snipping of the scissors stopped, glances were exchanged, pinups on the walls were admired but no one said a word. In the mirror the rain fell beyond the salon door, luminous under a streetlight. I suspected this stranger to be a policeman in mufti and was extremely grateful to Navaz Sharif for introducing me as his client. Maybe a jeep waited in the street, though I didn't have the faintest clue of the charges that were going to be framed.

'Make the whiskers smaller,' I instructed the hairstylist, just to underline my role as a client. 'Not much smaller, just a bit smaller.'

'You know us?' Navaz Sharif asked him, ignoring my instructions. 'How come?'

'I know you,' he said, with a nod which suggested he knew each of us. 'Why shouldn't I? I live right here in the mohalla. My name is Qadir.'

'Where do you live?' Navaz Sharif asked, putting away the pair of scissors and the pretence of cutting my hair.

'What do you want us to do?' demanded Zulfikar, trying to silence Navaz Sharif with a hand held up in the air, thus trying to brand himself as the leader of the gang.

'Something you have done before,' Qadir said. 'Something that involves vehicles. But on a much larger scale.'

Once again glances were exchanged, pinups were frowned upon, toenails were stared at but no one spoke for a while.

'Car loan recovery?' Jinnah asked finally. 'For ICICI or HDFC?'

'See,' Qadir said. He now stood with his elbows on the back of a barber's chair, making it squeal with the measured movements of his hands. 'I can't give you more information until you tell me if you want to do this.'

'Fair enough,' I said. He could be anything but a policeman in disguise. He held my gaze in the mirror for a moment. Then he nodded at my reflection.

'We want to discuss this amongst ourselves,' Zulfikar said.

'I want you to discuss this amongst yourselves and say yes or no next Sunday.' He turned to leave, eyeing the rain distastefully for a moment.

'How do we contact you?' Zulfikar held a hand out. 'Mobile number?'

'Don't worry. I will contact you. We will meet here on Sunday night?'

'Perfect,' Zia said.

'You have three days. I think there is enough time for you to make up your mind.'

'Perfect,' Zia said.

Then Qadir went out of the shop and walked into the rain, beginning to half-trot towards Franklin, when a flash of lightning lit up the sky above the outline of minarets.

If you are a practising Muslim living
in Vanity Bagh, you are a page in my ledger.
– Kareem Jabbari (1953-)

According to the imam's ledger, which had grown to the size of a busy tailor's book of measurements, five practising

Muslims by the name of Qadir lived in Vanity Bagh. Two had already kicked the bucket. One was too old to be our man, the other had been born only last Christmas. The remaining Qadir lived on the fringe of Vanity Bagh, where the cemetery of St Francis Basilica began, but had his business running from the mohalla's private little Nariman Point. If the ledger was anything to go by, he was a florist, a job that was a bed of roses when compared to the uncertainties and adventures that marked the career of loan recovery agents.

Looking up some girl's address?
When can I expect her mother here?
– Bushra Jabbari (1962-)

There was something fishy about this man. You could be a scrap dealer and a hooligan at the same time. Or a civil contractor and a contract killer. Or a restaurateur and a pimp. Or even a policeman and a pirate. But a florist doubling as a debt recovery agent was as unimaginable as orchid plants springing water lilies.

'He looks like a perfect crook,' I, based on my little research and analysis of the imam's ledger, observed.

'So do the six of us,' was Zulfikar's reply to this.

We decided to spy on the florist and they picked me for the job, mistaking my access to the imam's ledger for immense talent for sleuthing. I took Jinnah's bicycle and stopped by Fatima's house to borrow her husband's helmet that had a grinning skull painted on the back.

The best fights are the ones we avoid.
– Jackie Chan (1954-)

Riding a bicycle down a bustling, narrow market street wearing a motorcycle helmet, I epitomized bad espionage. People studied me with confused interest, even the suspect looked up from a heap of flowers when I pedalled past his shop.

The best way to describe the market is to compare it to an anaconda that has just had dinner. It has a modest mouth beginning from the side of Akbar Electricals, snaking narrowly through the mohalla to a point where it suddenly becomes a spacious oval patch, then narrowing as abruptly as it has widened and petering out to a mere tail which ends on Purana Masjid Road.

Qadir's shop was just beyond this belly-of-the-anaconda, it sat at a bend after which there were only fish stalls. The florist appeared to be there not to make money, but on a selfless mission to give the market-goers a whiff of fragrance before the stench of fish invaded their nostrils. His little shop, so vivid with colours, made you realize how monochromatic underwater life was. After the pleasing shades of Mangobagh's flora, all the seas had to offer was either steely grey or greyish black. In two days I did several helmeted rounds of the market, and Qadir looked briefly up every time my bicycle rattled past him, his profile framed either in the loop of a wreath or in the near oval of a garland, both meant for the day's commerce.

Then Sunday dawned, then Sunday brightened, then it dimmed and finally darkened. Khan Hair Salon remained open well past its closing time, Yahya posted on the steps to ward off drunks or perfectly sober human beings who, spotting the salon still open, might wander in for a haircut.

The *Titanic*, which had long sunk to the bottom of television ratings, had just hit the iceberg when Qadir finally rode up on a rickety Lambretta the colour of kadak tea. He left it on the pavement, where it stood with its headlight angled towards the salon as if it were keeping an eye on its master. Yahya came in and closed the door. Navaz Sharif switched off the television.

'Sit down, sit down,' Qadir said, as if he owned the shop, its three barbers' chairs, four visitors' chairs and one bench that had served three generations of clients. 'Have you made up your mind?'

'Yes,' Zulfikar said.

'Okay, you are saying yes?' Qadir asked.

'No,' Zulfikar said.

'No is what you have decided?'

'Listen,' Jinnah said. 'We can say yes or no only after you tell us what the job is.'

And he told us.

If our maiden operation had us taking possession of a car, this one would have us getting rid of scooters. We would not have to steal anything. We would just ride the scooters to the addresses Qadir would furnish us with. We would park them at specified places and just walk away. We would be carriers. That meant Qadir was not a loan recovery agent.

'This is drug business?' Zia asked, already expressing his unwillingness for the job with a shake of his head.

'This is gold business,' Qadir replied. 'There will be gold bars hidden in each scooter you ride to where we want them to be ridden. But the gold is not your responsibility. If you are followed or intercepted, you can ditch the scooter and escape. That's the standard norm we follow.'

We did not know gold smuggling had standard norms,

that the rules had been formulated by such golden-hearted dons.

'But we will not tolerate cheating,' Qadir said darkly.

'Neither will we,' replied Jinnah.

Qadir burst out laughing and seemed to want to thump Jinnah on the back but then settled for a few slaps on the countertop. 'I like you people,' he said. 'And I like the fact that you kept an eye on me for the last three days. In this business, if you walk with an open eye you go far. Now, yes or no?'

We looked at each other, and Qadir looked from face to face, expecting us to shout yes like schoolchildren. Our reluctance appeared to worry him beyond reason, and when we remained silent for longer than he had expected, he said, in a tone that suggested he had already given up, 'I am just asking you to do some valet parking for me. Only that you don't have to wear any funny uniform and bow at people when they grudge you paltry tips. No, Zulfikar?'

Zulfikar gave him a shy smile and a nod of agreement – his stint in valet parking at Residency Plaza had proved to be a sour experience for him and a sourer one for the hotel. A luxury sedan had suffered a mangled radiator grille and powdered headlamps in his hands, but this qualified him to speak with some amount of authority on the accuracy and infallibility of airbag deployment.

I have no idols. I admire work,
dedication and competence.
– Ayrton Senna (1960-1994)

'I don't know what stops you from saying yes. We have

options. We can always hire gangs from Begum Bazaar area to do this. But they are professionals, hence easy suspects for the police. You are not on police records. And you are all jobless. Now, yes or no?'

I thought what Qadir had said was the least persuasive thing I had ever heard in my life so I was immensely surprised, even a bit disappointed, when Zulfikar, after having glanced around the room, said, 'Deal.'

Close to an hour later, when Navaz Sharif switched on the TV after seeing off Qadir, the Titanic had completely sunk. Little did we know then that our own boat had started to roll, that we would soon run into an iceberg and get flung into a cold sea. And sink.

Navaz Sharif went around the shop snapping off lights, and finally he pressed the button on the remote and killed the TV. In the dark, someone heaved a sigh. It could have been anyone but Yahya. Yahya never sighed, you know?

XV

My son, whom you've called a bomb expert,
is scared of even those tiny, ten-per-rupee crackers.

~ Salma Auntie (1968-   )

No news from home. No sign of Ammi. It is already late October and it has been over a month since I last saw her cry. I have a list of probable reasons that keeps her away. A list that keeps growing day by day.

Probable reason 1: Wasim. Has he had a relapse? And is he back in the CCU of Shahbaz Memorial Hospital?

Probable reason 2: Abu Hathim sahib. Have his kidneys finally failed him completely? Did the ambulance that rushed him to the hospital with a rotating beacon and a shrieking siren finally drive back to the mohalla, sluggish and silent? Ammi, devastated by the news, knows it will leave me even more devastated.

Probable reason 3: Fatima's husband. Latif had broken a tower of crockery in his kitchen at the news of my arrest.

He banned Fatima from calling on Ammi and the imam, and referred to us as a family of terrorists whenever it pleased him. Has he threatened to send Fatima home if Ammi doesn't stop visiting me?

Probable reason 4: Zia. Could it be that Ammi does turn up on visitors' days without fail but is denied permission as an act of revenge for the blow Zia has dealt the jail? Four wardens have been suspended. The deputy superintendent has been transferred. A lookout notice has been published. The branch of the banyan where Zia sat holding the make-up man's phone has been sawn off. The October 2nd celebrations have been cancelled. My worktable got searched and I still get stared at.

Probable reason 5: Shoulder dislocation. Which Ammi is occasionally prone to.

Probable reason 6: October. The month that takes the imam out of Mangobagh. He joins a small band of mullahs on a six-city tour in the name of the Tabligh Conference while poor Ammi does double duty. Now, with Wasim indisposed, triple duty.

Probable reason 7: November. The month that once shook the city and has been in the news ever since, remembered with pictures of mangled metal, broken windows, blood-splattered walls and panel discussions on TV.

Probable reason 8: I have no clue. I am still thinking about reason 8.

For the books of empty leaves, I have found a new bookmark. It doesn't look as good as the feather; it doesn't look even half-good. But my new bookmark has more value: it carries the autograph of the king of sound engineering, who actually shook hands with Will Smith and was even half-hugged by him.

I don't watch movies.
But I'm happy that India has won three Oscars.
– Kareem Jabbari (1953-)

If truth be told, most of the inmates don't know who Will Smith is, nor do they care a damn about the king of sound engineering. The scraps of paper they had stood with in the sweltering sun were thrown away almost as soon they were elaborately autographed. I don't know if the king of sound engineering had a glimpse of his signature being balled up and tossed away. If he did he would have ranked it as the biggest insult of 2011.

So an autographed piece of paper is my new bookmark. I remove it from a 200-pager and look at the pages that are blank except for the blue rules on them. These days I imagine weird things about libraries. One of them is a library stocked only with books of blank pages. You borrow books on the merit of their binding, take them home and read from their blank pages the very stories you have always wanted to write but never knew how to begin. I am very impressed with this impossible idea of mine.

This ten-year-old Imran is very creative.
Boy, try poetry and do the mohalla proud. The way I did.
– Shair Shoukath (1928-2010)

Another weird imagery I have thought up recently has

something to do with calendars. It is a calendar with only eleven months on it. October blends into December with ease, and there is nothing to suggest that there once used to be November in between. I dread November. Maybe that's why I see November when I open the notebook to read from my own unwritten memoirs. It's only natural for us mortals to keep seeing what we would give anything to erase the memory of. There is one more thing I am afraid of and obsessed with at the same time. It is the number 11. So when I open a book, there it is, the number 11, a whole chapter of it.

November is the coolest month.
Flowers are lilac and memories are green.
– Shair Shoukath (1928-2010)

Eliot would be turning over in his grave.
– Professor Suleiman Ilahi (1949-)

Let us dissolve the Poetry Club.
That would be our biggest contribution to poetry.
– Rustom sahib (1951-)

The month, as I already said, was November. The date, as fate would have it, was 11. That makes it 11/11. You get the drift of the story I am reading? The day was overcast. It had poured overnight and, as the combination of rain and tin imitated the sound of distant artillery over our heads, Zulfikar's phone began to ring and vibrate.

He let it ring for a while, sniffing and swallowing, and

when he took the call he listened with serious distaste, as if something he had always dreaded would happen had finally happened. Then he hung up, dropped his head and nipped his eyebrows where they were conjoined.

'We will meet Qadir at 11 tomorrow.'

That, in hindsight, makes it 11/11/11.

But we reached the florist's five minutes late, and Qadir was waiting impatiently for us outside the shop. Without pleasantries or handshakes, he led us to the belly-of-the-anaconda area where three scooters were parked in front of a shop with its wooden shutters plastered over with several layers of film posters. One of them was the tea-coloured Lambretta, and all of them had new number plates, which meant they were fake numbers.

'Scooter No. 2342 will go to the Holy Cross Hospital parking lot,' Qadir said.

In Mangobagh, people are obsessed with the belief that the number plate of your vehicle can make or break your life; they have a simple way to decide if a vehicle is blessed with a lucky number, or cursed with an inauspicious one. They separate the digits of the registration number with an addition sign and add up all four digits to get a sum that could be even and lucky, or odd and ominous. That was what I did to the number of the scooter Qadir instructed to be ridden to a hospital. The sum of 2+3+4+2 was 11.

That makes it 11/11/11/11.

'Scooter No. 1901 will go to the bus bay next to Central Theatre.'

The sum total was 11 again. That makes it 11/11/11/11/11.

'And Scooter No. 2243 will go Vinayak Super Store.'

That makes it 11/11/11/11/11/11.

Then, in a lowered voice, Qadir instructed Zulfikar, who, as if picking a side for an evening match in the alley of Abu Hathim sahib's bungalow, assigned us tasks.

Zia and Navaz Sharif would ride to Holy Cross.

Jinnah and Zulfikar would take the Lambretta to the bus bay.

Yahya and I would go to Vinayak Super Shop.

Then he changed his mind; Jinnah would go alone. He would stay with the florist and function as the control room. His mobile phone number would be our helpline number. Call for any clarification.

And we rode off.

Vinayak Super Shop is the kind of supermarket that boasts of selling you anything other than your blood relations. It is old and sprawls over two badly lit floors, but the shelves are always full and the aisles crowded. It stands on the main road, fourth block from the intersection after the Air India building, with a popcorn machine and a Coke fountain under its extended awning. We were to park the scooter just outside the store and get out of the street, leaving the key behind; twenty minutes later someone would take possession of it, and an hour later we would get paid at the florist's.

The scooter clanked all the way to Mehendi, like someone had attached a tail of old tins to its rear number plate. I rode as fast as the rickety scooter would allow me, dreading that it would disintegrate into a pile of nuts and bolts and rusted coils in the middle of the road, leaving Yahya and I standing over the iron carcass as traffic roared and honked all around us.

Yahya sat stiffly behind me, his hands placed lightly on my hips as if he were to lift me up by the waist and start waltzing the moment music commenced. Strangely enough, the pathetic state of the scooter was the only thing that kept me worried on our three-mile journey to Mehendi. I was sure that we were not going to be caught; the only folly we were going to commit that afternoon was parking the scooter in front of Vinayak Super Shop with no intention of buying anything from them, besides the bigger folly of being Muslims and hailing from Vanity Bagh. But I had a Hindu name handy, and that would be my passport to any part of Mehendi. There was no question of being exposed as long as I refused to crack because Yahya's sign language would be too much for a stranger to paraphrase.

The light was red at the Begum Bazaar intersection. I casually glanced at a car that had tinted glasses, and caught my slightly distorted reflection in one of the windows. And for the first time in a very long time I remembered my first day in school, and the preparations for it. Ammi had riotously powdered my face and run a pencil over my eyebrows before slinging a sand-coloured satchel over my shoulder. The imam took me down the alley with a full smile he wanted to reduce by a few watts but looked unable to. We crossed the street after Mogul Bakery and ambled along the road until we were in the next street. Puddles were full and plenty; the imam held up a hand to signal caution to the driver when a vehicle approached. The school looked exactly like the ones illustrated in R. K. Laxman's cartoons: an arched gateway propped up on two lichened pillars, a spatter of rambling trees in the foreground and behind them a loose clutter of buildings the colour of my satchel. The imam daubed at my face with the end of his jubbah to reduce the effect of a mime artist the coat of talcum powder had given me and, with a smile of humility and a hand pressed to his heart, handed me over to a teacher. A moment later he slipped away without a formal wave of goodbye. But I caught him peeping through a window, checking to see if tears had smudged my face.

The red light turned to orange, then to green. And the scooter began to clamour threateningly again. Barely a quarter kilometre later the light was red at the Rajamata Colony intersection too. I kept the scooter growling, impatient to be out of the last busy junction before our destination. An auto rickshaw came to a halt beside us, crammed with kindergarten children, its roof loaded with colourful satchels secured with what looked like fishing nets. They eyed us suspiciously, then broke into wide grins as Yahya pretended to be a monkey and picked fictitious lice from my hair. It was like my memories moved with the traffic lights, and I remembered how my first day at school had ended. I had cried until I started to retch, and my eyes were bloodshot and body weak by the time school dispersed. The imam took me home on his shoulders, stopping by Mogul Bakery to bribe me in advance for the next day.

When the light changed, the auto rickshaw competed with us for a while, the children waving and howling at us. Then I slowed down, and let it trundle away. The Air India building was already in view, the sun glowing faintly on its weathered white tiles.

Mehendi was as sleepy as ever. The parking lot of Vinayak Super Shop was only half-full and, thankfully, unmanned. It was too early for shoppers to come, and the man at the snack stall under the cloth awning was just knotting the threads of his red apron behind his back, an act that reminded you of a woman struggling to fasten the hook of her brassiere, but the ice-cream counter was already open and had two young boys running their tongues over individual pink scoops.

Yahya slid off the scooter and wandered to the side wall of the next building, where he stood hugging himself, studying the fluorescent green posters of *Matrix II*. His interest appeared to be so complete that I could not help marvelling at his talent to be indifferent. I dragged the Lambretta onto its stand and strolled out of the parking lot, a hand fiddling with my zipper as if I were looking for a place to piddle. I was walking away from Yahya, towards the bus stop a few blocks down, where he would join me a few minutes later. Only when I crossed the street and was a few feet from the bus shelter did I realize that I had disobeyed Qadir's orders and committed a mistake. In my efforts to look casual, I had detached the key from the scooter and put it in my trouser pocket. Yahya, who was beginning to walk, paused to watch me retrace my steps to the parking lot and fiddle with the scooter. A shop assistant stared blankly out of a window as I pushed the key back into the ignition and walked unhurriedly away, past the bus stop, past a tiny petrol station, across a faded zebra crossing, around the Air India building and into an angular network of pocket roads which, if you walked into without looking back to see if you were being followed, brought you to the backyard of Vanity Bagh in twenty-five minutes.

About half an hour later, the birds of Mehendi flew off from their perches as a scooter went off with a bang that was soon to be codenamed 11/11.

XVI

Imran Jabbari suffers from a chronic mental illness.
I treated him once.

~ Dr Faud Niyazi (1966-)

It is already December on the wall calendar, and it has been easily two-and-a-half months since Ammi has stopped visiting. *Why*, I ask myself every Wednesday as inmates get summoned to the Visitors' Room, and the list of probable reasons for her absence grows in length and complexity.

Probable reason 9: Ammi herself. Is she finally sick of jail visits?

Probable reason 10: Mehendi Hind Sabha. Have they warned her against the visits through an anonymous letter?

Probable reason 11: Jail-o-phobia. Which is a horrible fear of going to jail even for a short period of time, though I am not sure if jail-o-phobia is the term it is referred to as in the dictionary.

Probable reason 12: Amnesia. She once claimed to have a huge memory loss, and we thought she was just acting up until Wasim asked her her name and she did not even remember that. The imam was seriously thinking about taking her to an ENT specialist when her memory was unexpectedly restored and she told Wasim her name was Bushra Jabbari. This happened many years ago, and cured itself before the imam had a chance to change his clothes. Has Ammi had a relapse?

Amnesia said hello to me.
I said I don't remember you. So off it went.
– Shair Shoukath (1928-2010)

Why don't you just cut me into little pieces
and feed me to the street dogs?
– Professor Suleiman Ilahi (1949-)

Me too, please.
– Rustom sahib (1951-)

Probable reason 13: Pregnancy. Fatima is pregnant again and needs twenty-four-hour looking after like last time?

On certain Wednesdays, the pilgrimage from the scot-free world comes in a long unbroken trail and inmate after inmate gets summoned to the Visitors' Room until the Book Room is empty except for a warden and me, and we sit like the orphans in the movie that left the king of sound engineering's family yelling and beating their chests in joy.

The warden usually walks away to a window and stands

there with his back turned to me. I invariably open a book and catch up on my reading.

Last Wednesday, I opened a book at random and found myself staring at a page oddly numbered 11/11. Ah, that is a custom-made coincidence.

A couple of years ago on 11/11, most of Mangobagh had clambered onto their roofs and looked southwards to see what had happened. But from a height it was impossible to distinguish between turmoil and tranquility. As they say, you need to come down to earth to comprehend life better, but when there are rumours about serial bombs collectively ticking away across the city, would anyone care to tread the streets without bomb suits?

The first news of the blast reached me at a quarter past one. I was lying on the bed, with a view of the long, murky passage that culminated in a doorway filled with brilliant sunlight and the occasional bleating of Ammi's two goats. I saw Wasim enter the house and stride down the passage; he dragged a chair from the table which served as the dining table, ironing board, study table and sewing machine stand at different times of the day, and started opening the lunch packet Ammi had packed for him in the morning. From the kitchen, Ammi asked why he was home early. Mouth already stuffed, he said something neither Ammi nor I could comprehend.

Then I heard Noora Auntie excitedly tell Ammi about a bomb blast. She had heard it on television and invited Ammi to watch the news as one of the channels was repeatedly airing her brother's eyewitness account of the blast.

'Where did this happen, Auntie?' Wasim asked, hurriedly washing his hands.

'Near Central Theatre, beta,' Noora Auntie said. 'Aurangzeb runs a paan shop next to it.'

'Ammi, I am going to Central Theatre,' Wasim yelled to the kitchen, drying his hands on a towel. 'Don't tell Abba.'

Ammi materialized in the passage with a ladle in her hand. 'Go and come back with a blown-off leg. And we can get two doctors to treat you. You are not going anywhere.'

'Let him come and watch our TV, Bushra,' Noora Auntie said.

Bickering, Wasim left for Noora Auntie's. A few minutes later, I hopped across the alley to a room full of people staring at a fourteen-inch television. Noora Auntie waved me in, though the man of the house was not particularly happy to see me. He always kept an eye on me when I paid them a visit.

It is strange, Imran. But whenever
you leave our home, so does something from our shelf.
– Abbas Chacha (1959-)

There was as much pandemonium in the room as on the television. The channel kept repeating what they labelled the first and exclusive visuals, and Aurangzeb's excited eyewitness account was a part of the exclusive package. Abbas Chacha wanted to flip the channel, but Noora Auntie wouldn't let him.

Finally, Abbas Chacha grabbed the remote from her and changed the channel. The new channel showed the same angle of devastation as the one in which Noora Auntie's brother had starred: a few burgundy benches, blood-splattered tiles, heaps of glass shards around an ice cream counter that had twisted window frames. Except for their logos, there was nothing to tell one channel from the other, as if the two cameramen had stood shoulder to shoulder and captured what the bomb and its capacity to change lives had left for them to capture.

Abbas Chacha kept flipping through the news channels. Same visuals, same tickertape, same excitement that left reporters fumbling for words at times. Then he stopped squeezing and shaking the remote and lingered on a channel which seemed to be more informed than other channels, though the visuals were much the same. There was a red circle on the screen, the kind that is liberally used to highlight things or people that suddenly deserve more attention than at the time they were caught on camera. The red circle that, when superimposed on a television image, instantly turns the subject into a culprit or an accomplice or a suspect or a victim. The ominous red circle started to flicker, as if to underline the importance of being a red circle, as the camera zoomed in on a scooter the colour of kadak tea.

For a moment I thought I had had a long siesta and was being treated to a tightly edited, nicely shot and amazingly sound-engineered dream. The moment passed, but nothing else did.

The scooter lay on its side, charred by the explosion and dripping with water from fire engines, its fake number plate still in place, disturbingly white amidst things singed and blackened. The reporter, with a finger pressed against her ear, was saying something, almost shouting, into the camera. I strained my ears to hear through the various sounds of the alley – sounds of hungry animals, of playing children and of clanking pots – and I heard the voice of the reporter, which bordered almost on childish excitement, say the bomb had been planted on this scooter that had mysteriously appeared in the locality around noon.

Abbas Chacha had started squeezing and shaking the remote again, and finally settled on the channel that had earlier featured his brother-in-law and now featured a newsreader who had the hairstyle of electrocuted people. The 'first and exclusive visual' label had disappeared; now it was 'Breaking News' galore on this channel. Big red stripes had taken over the lower half of the screen, and the newsreader kept repeating the word 'terror'. In the last fifteen minutes, two more bombs had gone off, one next to Holy Cross Hospital, the other in the parking lot of a supermarket in Mehendi. All were scooter bombs.

Give me a call at the first sign of trouble.
Don't waste even a second.
– Zulfikar Faizudin (1984-?)

I dialled his number. His phone rang thrice. Then the call was rejected. I dialled again. This time it was switched off. I tried Jinnah's number, and a recorded voice said all lines on that route were busy at the moment. The voice seemed to suggest that no matter how insistently I tried, I was not going to reach anyone that afternoon.

A bomb not only kills people directly,
but it kills them indirectly too.
– Public Prosecutor (-)

The scooter bombs killed eleven people directly. One of them was Jinnah. He had parked the Lambretta at the bus bay next to Central Theatre Complex and, instead of rushing back home, hung around a tea stall to spy on the cartel that dealt in gold bars. With such an insatiable urge to know what was forbidden, he must have been willing to wait for any stretch of time to have a glimpse of the next carrier in the network. He didn't have to wait for long; two cups of tea, one-and-a-half cigarettes and a loud bang later he was seen moving on all fours, blood gushing out of his mouth and falling between his hands as he crawled along the pavement to a roadside water tap, his tongue hanging out. An old clerk, who later tearfully recounted the last moments of a young man before Jinnah's involvement was suspected and investigated into, kneeled by him and made him drink from his water bottle. Jinnah gulped down every drop the bottle had to offer, then sat against a tree with a look of immense relief and died.

Neither the public prosecutor nor the police can tell you about the number of deaths the bombs caused indirectly. I think it is just a symbolic way of putting things, but the trouble with a symbolic way of putting things is it can impress people, including a judge. The more they impress a judge, the longer you spend in jail.

I often think about the call I made to Jinnah after coming out of Abbas Chacha's house. A recorded voice had said all the lines on that particular route were busy at the moment. If the lines were not busy and Jinnah's phone had rung, who would have picked it up? What would have been the words the stranger, possibly a policeman, said? *You called a bit too late. Sorry.*

I tried calling Zulfikar a third time, but it yielded the

same result as the second time. Then I dialled Navaz Sharif's number. To my surprise, he answered the phone as soon as it started ringing. There was the sound of the TV in the background, the faint hum of traffic and the snip of scissors. He said it was a busy day at the salon, that he would return the call when the shop closed. I asked him about Zia, and he said he had not met any of our friends for a couple of days. It was then that I remembered that call register had become the sniffer dog of the modern world; it would scurry invisibly along roads, leap from one mobile phone tower to the next, sneak down unsuspecting lanes and alleys and lead the police to a suspect. Could they already have begun tapping phones in Vanity Bagh since the bombs had been planted in predominantly Hindu areas? I thought it was too early to record telephonic conversations; they would get down to phone tapping only after rummaging through everything, including garbage, around the city with bomb detectors. Or would they have a software which would automatically tap all phones the moment bombs went off like chain crackers? Was Navaz Sharif talking just for the recording software, building up an alibi? If he was, so would I. I told him I had been ill all of last week and was still being treated by Dr Faud Niyazi.

Bring me people who have fitness
or sickness to prove. They get a certificate.
You get a commission, Imran.
– Dr Faud Niyazi (1966-)

Halfway through my sickbed story, Navaz Sharif heaved a sigh and hung up. And now I felt I was as ill as I pretended to be. All of a sudden I had a blocked nose, a sore throat and a heart that did not beat any longer. I walked up the street looking for … I didn't know who I was looking for. I would have been happy to see anybody from our gang, happier if it was Yahya. But I dreaded running into people who would tell me there had been a serial blast, that hundreds of people were blown to death, thousands injured. In the quickly failing light of Mangobagh winter, I bumped into no one I knew. At sunset I found myself sitting on the stairwell by the mosque, suddenly calm, waiting for them to shuffle up the stairs to repent.

It was here, sitting alone on the cold steps, that I regained enough composure to align the events of the day carefully like fossils. A slow reconstruction which left me more confused, more clueless. It all appeared to have happened a long time ago; in a matter of a few hours everything had turned as vague as an old memory. I felt I had long lost touch with my accomplices, who had become untraceable owing to the years that had passed since the bombs had gone off. The chimes of a clock, as if to hand me a better sense of time, seeped out through the windows of the mosque. It was seven; just about as many hours since the first bomb had tested the tenacity of Mangobagh's shock absorbers.

I lit a cigarette and replayed the rattling ride I had taken through the heart of the old city. I had stopped at an intersection and studied my face in the tinted glass of a car; I had stopped at the next intersection as well and children had waved and howled at us; I had ridden parallel to a family of four travelling on a motorcycle – that afternoon, I could have been the messenger of death for many.

The prayer hall began to fill up, the speakers on the minarets started to hum with the imam's singsong prayers. Then the prayer hall emptied, the pious went out to the street and the priest started latching the windows. It was a long time after the mosque's last light had been switched off that I spotted a figure plodding down the path that led to the foot of the stairs. I didn't recognize Jinnah until he had climbed the stairs and stood leaning over me with his hands on my knees.

'Where are the other chooths?' he asked.

'You are the first chooth to turn up today,' I said.

'Come on, let's go to the rooftop,' Jinnah said. 'I heard the police have switched on searchlights. As if the next bomb would come from the sky.'

Not knowing that Jinnah had died that afternoon, I followed him up the stairs. A long bar of light swept across the sky, illuminating nothing besides itself. Standing shoulder to shoulder, we peered down at Vanity Bagh.

'Look, there is your old heartthrob.' Jinnah was pointing towards the row of stalls behind Franklin.

'Where,' I asked. 'Who?'

'At the chaat shop,' he said. 'Aasia Jamal.'

'I will kill you.'

XVII

Imran Jabbari pleads insanity.
~ Defence Lawyer (1965-   )

Wasim was the first to notice the coincidence. I think he made the discovery even before the press did. Technically speaking, all newspapers quoted my brother the next morning, word for word, though no journalist was around when he returned from Noora Auntie's house and exclaimed aloud, 'It's 11/11.'

Was 11/11 just a coincidence or a well-hatched plot, nobody knows till date. But the mohalla-wallahs discussed theories by the dozen in their free time, and they had all the free time in the world.

Hilal Hathim, grandson of Abu Hathim sahib and first-born of the slain Rasool Hathim, celebrated his eleventh birthday on that very November 11. But would Abu Hathim sahib, though he had sworn revenge on the spur of the moment, celebrate a fatherless child's birthday with a bloodbath? The mohalla flung that stupid theory out of the window and drew the curtain.

Someone revenging for Yasser Arafat's assassination?
He died on November 11.
– Shair Shoukath (1928-2010)

Don't be silly. Arafat died a natural death.
– Professor Suleiman Ilahi (1949-)

No, professor, he was slow-poisoned.
And Shoukath miyan, limit your imagination to poetry.
– Rustom sahib (1951-)

While the papers were read and theories were formulated, debated and discarded, Jameela Auntie put her head around our door and asked if we had seen Jinnah. He had not come home last night, his mobile phone was dead. She had looked up every place he could possibly be. Even, she said with tears welling up in her eyes, the police station.

'The biggest favour some people can do their families is vanish,' the imam said from the armchair. Jameela Auntie looked helplessly at Ammi, who glared at the imam, flaring her nostrils, and for a moment I didn't put it past her to take down a porcelain bowl from the cupboard and break it into two unequal parts on the imam's head.

'Take Imran with you,' she instructed Jameela Auntie. 'He sure knows more of Jinnah's hangouts than you and I do.'

We were clomping down the alley to the main street when Jameela Auntie remembered something and signalled me to stop. 'Where does that dumb idiot live?' she asked. 'Jinnah said yesterday he was going somewhere with him.'

'You mean Yahya, Auntie?'

'Yes, the same idiot.'

Yahya lived in a house of pockmarked wood and dimpled tin in a slum-like settlement leaning against the back wall of Bukhari Mills. Jameela Auntie looked unpleasantly at the narrow, miry path, curtained with the day's laundry, which rolled endlessly away in twists and turns. As we pushed our way down the path that was too narrow to let two people walk side by side, I heard the sound of the television filtering out through walls that were nearly as flimsy as packing boards. (The only household in the mohalla that took the imam's preaching against television seriously was his own, ours.)

'Stop,' Jameela Auntie said. 'Is that the place?' She was pointing at the house that looked like the remains of a catastrophe waiting to be rebuilt.

'Yes.'

'Why is there a crowd?' she asked. 'And why is the Quran being recited so early in the morning?'

What struck me as strange was not the sound of verses rendered in a forced nasal tone, but the abundance of electric bulbs that shone in every room, as if the house was getting ready for a photo session.

Lights are a building's make-up.
Especially if you are going for an exterior shot.
– Javed Miandad (1980-)

An elderly couple came out of the house and walked quietly past us, the man holding my gaze for a second, the woman nodding sympathetically at Jameela Auntie. 'Someone is dead, Imran,' Jameela Auntie whispered. 'Go and find out who.'

I took a few strides and stopped; I was dressed in a fake

Armani T-shirt and a pair of jeans with one knee threadbare, the other riotously torn. It would be rude to enter a house of death thus dressed. Just inside the rusted, permanently open gate was a willow tree; I blended into a small band of old men beneath it and spied on the house of no particular shape. Yahya's father, who looked exactly like Kofi Annan from certain angles, sat in the veranda with his head propped up in his hands; he looked up every time a mourner passed him, and tried to get up but was discouraged by a man, perhaps his brother, who looked like Morgan Freeman.

Under the willow tree, the old men chatted away in mild accusatory whispers, though they were not even remotely critical of anybody. Eavesdropping on them convinced me that Yahya had not left a suicide note behind. The oldest of the lot said the boy was depressed over his speech impairment. The youngest suspected him of falling out with his father and taking his life on an impulse which could have been easily tackled if the victim had practised yoga. A third one asked if he had a drug problem. A fourth one asked if anyone had a cigarette. But none suspected Yahya of being an indirect victim of a bomb blast.

Then, like everywhere else, the conversation under the willow tree steered itself towards 11/11.

If you spot any suspicious object, please call the control room.
Our number is 111. Sorry, I mean 101.
– Commissioner (-)

If anybody harboured any suspicion about Vanity Bagh's involvement in the serial two-wheeler bomb blasts, it was only the mohalla-wallahs. But the mohalla suspected itself only in murmurs. Even Mehendi thought it was beyond Vanity Bagh to design and plant scooter bombs. For them, we were nothing more than a poor neighbourhood that was home to petty criminals, infamous conmen and an extortionist who successfully repackaged himself as Robin Hood. Terrorists we could never be. We could build roadblocks and run riots at the drop of a hat, turn the public transport system into mobile billboards carrying inflammatory headlines and taglines and transform peace rallies into a scene from *Karate Kid 2*, but handling serial blasts was something else. It needed planning and precision, virtues Mehendi would hate to credit our mohalla with.

On the second day after the blast, the police released my composite sketch. If you wonder how accurate a police drawing could be, I would give it three on ten for accuracy; Yahya would have given the sketch the kind of rating that could have either made the artist tender his resignation or initiate legal action against him for defamation. The only person the sketch bore any resemblance to was Mohammed Atta of 9/11 fame. But how did a funny moustache, which neither Atta nor I had thought of cultivating, find its way into the picture? They had done my portrait after intently listening to the shop assistant who had seen me sitting on the scooter. Four Atta lookalikes were picked up, interrogated and let off – they were either Hindus or had strong alibis.

On the third morning, Jameela Auntie, accompanied by a corporator, walked into Begum Bazaar police station to lodge a complaint for man-missing. She carried a cabinet-sized picture of Jinnah posing against somebody's Audi A8, beckoning the world with a finger to get into what he pretended was the latest addition to his already impressive fleet. It took the police just two hours to half-crack the case and one day to trace the roots of the serial blast to Vanity Bagh. The fourth morning the NIA came, hunting for unusual suspects.

The passive fourth morning was preceded by an eventful third night. Late into the night, just as Navaz Sharif was snapping switches off in preparation for shutting the salon, three hefty men trooped in and asked for crew cuts. Grabbing his mobile phone, Navaz Sharif made for the dark street, but they caught him at the swing doors and dragged him back to the wall of mirrors, where he was forced into a chair and asked to apologize. He readily said sorry, which was construed not just as an act of expressing regret, but a confirmation of his role in the blast. The heftiest of the three opened a drawer and took out a tube of shaving cream and a brush. He opened another drawer and fished out a shaving razor as well. As he whipped up lather on a plastic bowl, he said he was going to give the barber a shave. Navaz Sharif could do well without his mullah beard; Mangobagh could do very well without another mullah. Then he pressed Navaz Sharif's head against the headrest of the chair and slit his throat.

On the fourth morning, the NIA drove up in a blue van with wire mesh windows, and picked up us one by one in strict alphabetical order. They didn't say 'Freeze, NIA' or anything more tempting; I noticed they even sacrificed the chance to flourish their ID cards in order to avoid hurting family sentiments. Two men casually strolled into the house and one of them took me by the wrist. 'Come with us,' the other one said. Had they been dressed up like ordinary constables, Ammi would have whined the roof down or even fainted. Reassured by the quiet ways of these full-sleeved, teacher-faced men, she remained composed and tight-lipped as they herded me out of her sight. One of them even wrapped a hand around my shoulder as we stepped out of the house; Ammi must have been greatly comforted by that unexpected gesture of camaraderie.

Next we stopped by Zulfikar's, where the plainclothesmen on duty walked up to the van to inform that the boy was still at large. The van was being reversed when the door of the house was flung open and Salma Auntie tumbled out with a yelp, palms glued together, hair all messed up. Fighting her way through a small crowd, she rushed to the van to stand between the plainclothesmen and lament through the wire mesh. She must have been sitting in the dark for long and was blinded by the sudden burst of harsh sunlight, for she mistook me for an NIA officer, and her words to me were so unexpected and bereft of uncertainty that they turned into a quote many a newspaper cared to print the very next day.

> If my son is the enemy of the nation,
> hang him. And don't even show me his corpse.
> – Salma Auntie (1959-)

> She is just playing Mother India.
> The drama queen! Abu Hathim's keep.
> – P. Mudassar (1960-)

Zia, who had emulated an ostrich by switching off his mobile phone and keeping indoors, was stepping out of his home when we pulled up by the construction site that overlooked the little republic that his joint family was. He was dressed in an Islamic cap and somebody else's clothes – a long white kurta and matching pajamas, and matching sandals. The kind of clothes the rich and the famous put on when they go for the funerals of the other rich and famous, though neither Zia nor Navaz Sharif was either rich or famous. The news of the murder in the salon had spread through the mohalla by sunset, though it would get its share of newsprint only the next morning, along with the news of our arrest.

Zia produced a pair of sunglasses from his pocket, puffed at their petal-shaped glasses, rubbed them against a sleeve and put them on. He instantly looked like a Page 3 item, and the NIA men agreed that the suspect could have been in the movies if he had not been in deep shit. 'Does your friend act?' asked one of them. When I nodded my head in the negative, he pulled a face and moaned.

Zia rolled up the sleeves of his borrowed kurta and sized up the lane. For a moment his eyes rested on the half-built structure and an idling carpenter, who had embraced carpentry only that morning to spy on Zia. He then looked at the duo of constables dressed up as masons, and strolled towards a bicycle shed. A man who had been daubing lime on a wall in the most amateurish way imaginable threw his brush away and trailed Zia. As Zia leaned over a bicycle to unlock it, the painter-inspector put a hand on his shoulder.

I think I missed something in between by blinking; the next thing I saw was Zia sprinting barefoot to a wall and a whole bunch of the construction crew chasing him. Beyond the wall was an incline dotted with thorny bushes sloping down to the old canal, an area Zia knew like the back of his hand. It gladdened me that he didn't make it.

He was carried to the van with a look of utter shock and a nosebleed; his sunglasses now had one empty frame, so that he appeared to be wearing an eyepatch. A little girl who had witnessed the chase and its conclusion had run to the joint family and brought all of them out onto the street.

When the back door of the van opened, Zia was surprised to see me inside.

'Come on, son,' one of the NIA men said. 'Have a seat.'

'And cheer up,' chipped in the other. 'Your entire family is here to see you off.'

Zia started to sob like a child who had been denied a ride down a slide.

As if to force poetic justice into the case, the trial was completed in eleven months. Qadir and Zulfikar were tried in absentia. Post-mortem reports of Jinnah, Yahya and Navaz Sharif were tabled to assure the judge that they were not going to come back and blow raspberries at him. The final verdict, to the delight of the bereaved and the press, was decided to be delivered on November 11. My only hope was the judge getting carried away with the overdose of 11 and slapping on me eleven months of rigorous imprisonment and 11K as penalty. I got fourteen years, Zia got six months more; he probably earned the extra retribution for making the police run around in their fancy dress costume. The imam, as anticipated, did not turn up. Ammi, as expected, fainted. She had attended every single session the fast-track court had held over the eleven months, sharing an auto rickshaw with Zia's parents and going Dutch. The defence lawyer, who had always looked like he was going to win the battle, walked up to us with a pout and mumbled regret.

Sorry. It's all over.
– Defence Lawyer (1965-)

Nothing is over. Nothing.
You just don't turn it off. It wasn't my war.
– Sylvester Stallone (1946-)

XVIII

My parents are old and ill. My brother is young and invalid. And I am their only hope.
~ Imran Jabbari (1985-   )

You can tell the heroes of an era by its notebook covers, unless you are looking at the ones made in this prison. The books we make here have the same cover design – yellow-and-purple concentric patterns that remind you of disco lights in old Hindi movies. I was not only bored by this design, I even had a few nice alternatives to suggest. Like this superlative one: the cover will afford an aerial view of a football field complete with all the positions of the players marked, or a cricket ground with a classic field setting with short descriptions. So you know the difference between a stopper-back and a midfielder, and you can tell a leg slip from a forward short leg. In their free time, kids can use their fingers to play a little game on top of their notebooks, a screw of paper for a cricket ball or a Cadbury gem for a Jabulani. I insist the view has to be aerial, otherwise it doesn't work. If they could put me through to the man in charge of designing, we could together bring more utility value to notebooks. They could even brand it. I can personally assure you it will sell like hot cakes. But procedures are silly and not simple in a prison.

On a Wednesday afternoon, when the inmates had left for the Visitors' Room and the Book Room was empty except for a friendly-looking warden and me, I put forth a proposal to him. He instantly stopped looking friendly. Knitting his eyebrows, he gave me the is-that-the-only-thing-that-concerns-you look. When I enlightened him on the branding part and made it more irresistible by saying he could claim to the superintendent that it was a combined brainwave of his and mine, his frown thawed to some degree of affability. But in the end he said all notebooks in the world now have the same design.

What? Are we living in an age of no heroes? Or, according to some new rules, you need to share the proceeds with the celebrity whose picture is on the cover? Then concentric circles make sense, as do floral patterns and Tetris blocks.

As inmates came in from the Visitors' Room one by one with scowls and sad smiles and I turned to go back to my worktable, the warden asked me why I don't get visitors anymore.

Probable reason 14: Alzheimer's. Ammi's Abba died of Alzheimer's disease, and until the day he died he mistook the imam for the man at the gas agency who took bribes from him but never honoured the promise of an additional cylinder. 'Where is my gas?' he kept asking, and the imam, the worst actor any two-legged creature could ever be, mimed complicated paperwork and signalled that the delivery truck had already left the warehouse and would be at his doorstep any time now. We ranked it as the top joke of the day every time we paid Grandpa a visit.

Abba, you have double gas trouble.

– Wasim Jabbari (1988–)

One thing I notice about books these days is that they have become tall and handsome. When we were in school, books were almost half the size of what they are now. And back then notebooks had only pages and binds, not screens and keypads. Most of my primary-school notebooks had Imran Khan on their covers, Wasim's had Wasim Akram. The imam used to source them from a stationery shop on Sufi Baba Road and was under the everlasting impression that the notebooks with our namesakes on the covers made us immensely popular at school. When we were given the freedom and money to choose our own notebooks, Wasim came back from the school store with Hulk Hogan in orange underwear; I simply invested the money in a jackpot venture a crook with infectious optimism ran outside the school.

Three weeks after I told the friendly-looking warden about the idea of notebook covers with sporting arenas as seen from the heavens, the superintendent, his new deputy (the old one had been transferred shortly after Zia had jumped the jail wearing his sunglasses), a head warden and the friendly-looking warden came into the Book Room. All were wearing their best smiles, or rather the superintendent was wearing his best smile, so the rest had no other option than to follow suit.

The head warden held up a hand in the air and said the superintendent had an announcement to make. So all those who were working stopped doing so, and those who were pretending to be busy now pretended to be all ears. The Book Room attained the silence of a library as the superintendent put a sheaf of papers on a table and prepared himself for a little speech; anybody who had watched enough news bulletins would know the superintendent's role model in oratory was the president of America. He touched the edges of the sheaf of papers he had in front of him, half-smiled to himself and waited for the right moment to begin. But when he opened his mouth to speak, all the practised poise quickly left him, and he ended up with the body language of one of those Arab dictators all American presidents equally want dead.

> The United States must get a taste of its own poison.
> – Saddam Hussein (1937-2006)

He used his hands without restraint, spoke with aggression and thumped on the table for attention when one of the inmates looked absently out of the window.

'Ladies and gentlemen,' he began, determined to make us laugh, and the men in khaki promptly acknowledged his sense of humour with a short burst of laughter. 'I don't know how many of you know the history of this room. The Book Room was the idea of Mr Iyengar from whom I took over the charge of this prison seven years ago. Seven years back the output of the Book Room was just 300 books a month. It climbed to 750 three years ago and has been steadily growing thanks to the concerted efforts of everyone concerned. And today I am proud to say that we produce an average of …' He paused to smile at the inmates the American-president smile, to make the number he was going to reveal sound bigger than it actually would be. Someone had already started to clap, but realizing that the achievement of the Book Room was yet to be quantified he pretended to be dusting his palms.

'… 2100 books per month.'

Applause from everyone, except the one who earlier had a false start.

'I repeat, 2100 books a month. In certain months it is much more than that.'

All of a sudden I felt overworked as a louder round of applause erupted in the room. Two inmates, who had been raking the earth around the banyan tree that had extended a helping hand to Zia and shoved him over the wall to the free world, stopped working and tilted their heads towards the sound of the applause. Then they came over to investigate, to see if what they had heard was the first sign of a prison revolt and they could be of any help to the winning side. Standing at a window they peered in, their faces lit up with smiles of expectation. The superintendent stopped talking, and his American-president composure once again degenerated into the antics of a despotic Arab.

> Those who do not love me do not deserve to live.
>
> – Colonel Gaddafi (1942–2011)

His face set with a what-the-fuck-is-happening-in-this-jail expression, the superintendent sized up his cortege, every member of which shuffled briskly in their boots, but it was the head warden who dashed to the door and, grabbing a wooden scale from a table on his way out, skirted the room on tiptoe like that nameless biped in Walt Disney cartoons. Then he was standing at the window behind the inquisitive inmates who were still trying to tune their eyes to the half-dark interior. We saw the scale rise in the air and fall, and one inmate jump up in the air and scamper away. The other deftly dodged the blow and sprinted towards the banyan tree, where he gathered a hoe in the run and started digging a hole in the earth without delay.

The entire Book Room was left in stitches for some time.

A day without laughter is a day wasted.
– Charlie Chaplin (1889-1977)

With a hand in the air, the superintendent requested silence. Compressing our lips, we complied.

'Now let me get on to the real matter. We have been using the same cover for our notebooks for the last ten years or so. And we have decided to change it.'

No one but I clapped.

'Nothing wrong with the old cover. But I am no expert to judge art. Nor am I an artist myself. But last month the principal of St Peter's, whose store buys about 40 per cent of the books we produce, said they were looking for a little more imaginative book covers. The reason being there are hardly any repeat sales after the first purchase, which school rules insist should be done only at the school store. They have identified, after a little research, the reason for the drop in sales to be the cover design. They are a bit serious. And who wants to have serious stuff these days.'

Someone yawned. But it had nothing to do with the superintendent's discourse. This particular person yawned every afternoon around this time.

'So the school has asked us to go a little imaginative on the cover. Something that would induce repeated purchase among its students. Our first idea was to run a competition among our inmates. The Best Cover Competition. Then I was told that we have a budding artist amongst ourselves.'

Everyone was looking at me. Or I imagined everyone was looking at me.

'I have always believed in giving opportunities to people. People who are unfortunate enough to live in prison and government servants who are fortunate enough to work with the jail department. Equal opportunities to everyone. No discrimination.'

If Zia was still around and had he been in one of his foulest moods, he might have quizzed the superintendent as to whether he could go home every evening like the wardens did.

'So last Sunday I had a chat with the principal and bounced off an idea that sounded very interesting to me. Father Isaac, who is very hard to please, loved it.'

Everyone applauded the idea that the hard-to-please Father Isaac loved.

'It is my pleasure to introduce you to this talented artist.'

Everyone was smiling at me. Or I imagined everyone was preparing themselves to smile madly at me.

'But before I introduce you to the creator, let me introduce you to his creation.' He whipped out two sheets from the sheaf and held them up like the pictures of a fugitive. 'They are not just notebook designs. They are tiny playfields.'

Everyone applauded the little playfields. The superintendent asked the sheets to be passed around the room. They had been impressively executed, what with the dual-toned grass turf and representative galleries skirting the pitch. I stole a glance at the friendly-looking warden. He cocked his head slightly to a side and winked at me almost imperceptibly, which equalled a thumbs-up sign given the fact that his superiors were around. The computer print-outs completed one full cycle and the superintendent was holding them again.

'Now, let me present to you the brain behind this little but very significant idea which will increase the Book Room output to nothing less than 2500 per month.'

I coloured the way I had not coloured since the imam caught me polishing my dick with his hair oil. I allowed myself a half-smile and lowered my eyes to my feet.

'And here is that little designer.'

I looked up at the superintendent with a smile of gratitude and found him standing with a hand on the friendly-looking warden's shoulder. 'He has been recommended for a double increment and will receive a certificate of merit from IG, Prisons.'

Everyone applauded the son of a bitch, who was now seeking the superintendent's permission to say a few words of gratitude. The permission to deliver as many words of praise as he could in two minutes was granted by the deputy superintendent.

'My 1001 thanks to Joseph sir. Joseph sir has always believed in giving opportunities to people. People who are unfortunate enough to live in prison and government servants who are fortunate enough to work with the jail department. Equal opportunities to everyone. No discrimination. Thank you.'

The head warden and the deputy superintendent exchanged glances, as if asking each other: *Haven't we actually heard this before? Or is this just déjà vu stuff?*

'One more thing. I dedicate these cover designs to Joseph sir who is retiring next week. Please accept this, Joseph sir. Thank you.'

Exactly a week later, a small convoy of government vehicles with red boards on their grilles rolled in through the prison gates, bringing the top brass of the jail department to bid farewell to the superintendent with bouquets and garlands. Decorations from the Independence Day celebrations had been dusted and hung around the Record Room like bitter memories. And the prison, once again, bore a close resemblance to my school. The prison officials, like teachers, strolled in and out of the Record Room carrying savouries on paper plates and tea in plastic cups; the superintendent, equalling the outgoing headmaster, looked dolefully out of the window; and the inmates, like students, were left alone to sit under trees or wander around buildings. At the back of the Record Room I spotted a stocky man with a camera slung around his neck, his hands laden with refreshments, his cheeks distended with a samosa. His eyes, shaded by the visor of a Nikon cap, lingered on me for a while before he relieved his hands of the paper plate and plastic cup and plodded across the wet mould that stretched under many trees like a designer rug. But not until he took off his cap did I recognize my old neighbour from Vanity Bagh.

'Javed Miandad,' I yelled. 'You have put on weight.'

'Imran bhai,' he yelled back. 'You have lost weight.'

On the brink of a bear hug we decided against it and shook hands. And once enough pleasantries were exchanged and enough smiles smiled, I began to rant about how I missed the mohalla, how I envied him for being able to go back after the farewell party to his tiny room above Haja Stores and stand at a derelict balcony above the colonnaded shops to watch traffic crawl down the road to the intersection, to smell the aroma of Arabic delicacies cooked at wayside stalls, to have a smoke and tea as the sun set behind Franklin and the biggest neon board on the street started bluffing about the century-old legacy of Akbar Electricals.

'Don't worry,' he said. 'I will show you a bit of the mohalla I have captured over the last few months,' Javed Miandad said.

Cradling the camera in his hands, he kept a red button pressed until a screen the size of a cigarette pack flashed to life with the sound of a sword being waved in the air. 'Stand behind me and look over my shoulder,' he said.

With each punch of the button the swish of a sword escaped the camera and, one by one, pictures flashed across the screen. But the angles were so dramatic and the pictures so hopelessly abstract that the subject could have been any goddamn place on earth. An orange sun cut into three unequal pieces by electric cables; a half-empty glass of tea placed on a patina-coloured stool; a dog sleeping in front of a rust-coloured shutter; snippets of an unsuspecting street captured from Javed Miandad's rundown balcony; and the aerial view of a funeral procession, of a green rattan casket submerged in a sea of white skullcaps against the backdrop of a tree that I recognized with some effort as the good old Franklin. I wondered whose last journey out of the mohalla it was, whose page in the imam's ledger had earned an amendment and whose death had finally brought glory to his life.

Something told me that Shair Shoukath lay inside the green casket, his shoulders knocking softly against the rattan planks in tandem with the unsynchronized movements of the people who carried the casket. Ammi had casually mentioned the demise of my favourite poet, and how the mohalla had mourned the irreparable loss of a voice that was so strong and original that the pseudo-intellectuals in the locality had indicted him with shameless plagiarism. No one outside the mohalla had ever said a word against him, for his verses and fame never travelled past the intersection to the south and the cemetery of St Francis Basilica to the north.

Radical poetry has lost its torchbearer.
Shair Shoukath will be greatly missed.
– Professor Suleiman Ilahi (1949-)

Without his contributions, the Poetry Club
would never have become what it is today.
– Rustom sahib (1951-)

Javed Miandad kept glancing over his shoulder to see if he was wanted inside the Record Room where something that should not be seen through a viewfinder was currently in progress. Maybe they had taken out something distilled in the backyard of the prison soon after the convoy of government vehicles had left the compound and begun drinking it or they were passing the hat around to give the superintendent an unofficial lump sum. His finger kept punching a button with clockwork precision, making pictures slide in and out of the screen.

Now I was looking at less dramatic pictures, though their appearance and disappearance were still marked by the same crisp swish of the sword.

'These are the pictures that buy me three square meals a day, Imran bhai. They are not a part of my portfolio.'

A man who looked like Morgan Freeman stood in front of a mike. A man who reminded you of Kofi Annan held up a trophy the size of a teacup. A boy who looked like the younger brother Yahya never had smiled from the stock floral vignette of a green badge. A frightfully small stage stood, lopsided, at the end of an alley I could not recognize. I asked Javed Miandad to go to the previous slide.

'Who is this?' I asked, pointing a finger at the boy on the badge.

Javed Miandad screwed up his eyes and shielded the screen with a hand against the glare of sunlight. 'Ah, it's Yahya. The dumb boy who committed suicide. He was your friend, no?' he said, looking over his shoulder once again. 'His family has started an annual mime competition in his memory. Sponsored by none other than Abu Hathim.'

Before I could jokingly ask him if one of my parents had won it every time, Javed Miandad stiffened beside me and his voice hardened, 'Just walk away from me, Imran bhai. A warden is watching us.' He glued an eye to the viewfinder and tilted his face to follow the flight of an imaginary bird.

I drifted away towards the bamboo clumps by the garden steps as a warden came down a gravel path to summon Javed Miandad back to the Record Room. The last time I looked back, he was on his knees, trying to take the best snap of the bird that the sky was completely bereft of.

The green badge and the boy at its centre stayed with me through the night. I dreamed of Yahya and woke up to the chirp of birds that lived in the trees in the courtyard, darting little sparrows I had started to think of as jailbirds. It was still dark outside, except for a bare electric bulb that dangled from the roof of a windowless expanse of lime-washed wall. I decided to stay up what remained of the night; sunrise couldn't be far away, else birds would not have started chirping.

I remembered standing under the willow tree, wearing a fake Armani T-shirt and a pair of jeans torn at the knees, listening to a bunch of old men while Jameela Auntie waited in the alley. The men spoke in mild accusatory tones, imparting no specific information about the death until a mourner, who had woken up late because he had stayed up late watching the aftermath of the bomb blasts on TV, joined them and asked rapid-fire questions. Who, when, how, where ... And one of the old men with a goatee that Humera and Tabu would die for narrated Yahya's final day as if he had witnessed it himself. Some old dicks have a penchant for spinning yarns, and they turn hearsay into convincing eyewitness accounts with ease. And this was what Goatee told the latecomer:

The afternoon Mangobagh's three streets rocked with bomb blasts and the rest with its reverberations, Yahya came home late for lunch. He was stuffing himself up hurriedly as if he had some important post-lunch appointments to honour when his father, as was the old man's weekly habit, started scolding the boy for frittering away his time like it were counterfeit money. The boy finished his lunch without resorting to sign language – which invariably ended with the third finger from the thumb moving up and down in the air – to answer his father, and settled on the sofa to watch the afternoon movie on TV. He loved English movies, especially ones that involved prisons or sacked FBI agents. The old man followed him to the narrow, dingy room where he continued spitting invectives on the boy, the likes of whom had been termed as the favourites of God by people like Mother Teresa. In spite of his Kofi Annan looks, the old man was probably the basest domestic villain in the area, and once he got himself started he couldn't stop until the neighbours intervened. This afternoon he wouldn't let the boy watch Ghost Rider *in peace, though the boy had already watched* Ghost Rider *thrice on Star Movies and twice on DVD. Sounding like a car horn that got stuck and kept blaring, he ranted on, calling the boy's five best friends the mohalla's shadiest characters, and accusing him of coming home just to eat, watch movies and sleep on the sofa thereafter. Would today's kids sit through such nonstop crap?*

Goatee was sure his own grandson Aamir would certainly not tolerate such heartless haranguing. In rage, the boy switched channels and kept staring at the screen until tears welled up in his eyes. After a while, tears streaming down his face, he stormed out of the house. The old one was still ranting when the boy returned with something wrapped in a newspaper and locked himself up in his room. Ten minutes later he came out of the room frothing at the mouth, clutching his stomach and moaning silently.

If you had spotted a taxi zipping through the mohalla with

the headlights blazing in broad daylight and the horn tootling nonstop, it was the boy's parents, an uncle and Goatee taking him to Shahbaz Memorial Hospital. It was a bad day to consume poison, because all the hospitals were bursting with the bomb blast victims. There was not even a wheelchair available, let alone a vacant bed. They spread a sheet in the passage outside the casualty wing and gave him first aid. But Goatee had already given him first aid in the car, a surah whispered into his ear. They said they would wash his stomach after ten minutes and asked them to keep talking to him. His parents could only cry, his uncle was on the phone; Goatee was the one who did all the talking. He kept telling the boy he was going to be all right though the boy didn't look good at all. He signalled to his mother for water, and she poured water into his mouth and verses into his left ear. At first he gulped it hungrily down, then his mouth filled up and water started streaming from the corners of his mouth. Goatee asked the lady to stop, but she kept on feeding him. Mother, no? Mothers love feeding kids, no? She couldn't believe that the boy had gone. The first thing Goatee did after coming back from the hospital was tell his children to handle their children with caution. Don't chide them beyond a point. Today's kids are suicidal. The funeral is after the zuhr prayers. At the Purana Masjid Kabristan.

And you, local Michael Jackson, don't ever visit a house of death
in torn clothes. Even if you are a ragpicker's son.

– Goatee (-)

The sun had risen above the prison wall; the jailbirds were hopping about in the courtyard as the sun touched the shingles with a feathery orange light.

XIX

This case will be remembered not for
the number of people convicted.
But for the number of people who could have been.

~ *City Journal* (1898-   )

The new superintendent looks much younger than his predecessor. He has big, sad eyes and no moustache, and has a habit of looking away when inmates smile at him. He probably thinks we are making fun of him for his young age and fleshy cheeks, for his quick stride and hairy hands. With his deputy and three head wardens in tow, he once breezed through the Book Room, fixing everyone with a hard stare as if each and every inmate were on his list of convicts to be dealt with an iron hand.

I think I saw one of the wardens whom Zia got suspended with his vanishing act back in action, briefing a batch of newcomers on the work rules of the prison under a tree. Each newcomer is like a backpacker, only that he misplaces his papers and gets embroiled in legal complications and long delays, and is destined to live in a nation that allows only two types of civilian clothes – khaki for the rulers, white for the ruled – until his papers are tracked down, cleared and stamped 'Exit'.

This twelve-year-old Imran is a rare talent. Look at his poem. Each mohalla-wallah is a tourist ...
– Shair Shoukath (1928–2010)

Running errands for you doesn't make anybody a poet.
– Professor Suleiman Ilahi (1949–)

Imran, keep writing. Thank you.
Shoukath, show some respect for poetry.
– Rustom sahib (1951–)

A few months after the trial began, Mehendi Hind Sabha started a campaign to press capital punishment for all the accused. In retaliation, Vanity Bagh set up Mothers against Noose, a movement that was born in one of the innumerable bylanes of the mohalla and, after a month of frenzied campaigning, buried not far from it. It was a young college girl who thought up the counterstroke, called it 'Mothers against Noose' and later unwittingly gave it the acronym 'MAN' which drained it of all its maternal sensitivities.

Motherhood is the most beautiful thing.
When a mother loses her child she stops being one.
– Mehreen Malik (1993–)

Noor Jahan sahiba, who had been drawn to the window

by a richly modulated and almost unbearably shrill voice, peeked cautiously down to see if a new villain had arrived in the alley to deliver to her family another instalment of their periodic misfortune. Finding that it was just a scrawny girl who could pose no threat to her family – not that girls could not be human bombs, but this one looked incapable of even passing wind unaided – she leaned over the window with a new apprehension: could this girl, especially since she was talking about the beauty of motherhood, have mothered one of her dead or living sons' offspring? If DNA tests, like the home pregnancy checks advertised on TV as a modern miracle, were as simple and could yield as instant results, she would have summoned the girl upstairs and had the necessary contraption pushed up wherever the manual said it should be pushed.

But this girl was not talking about her sons. The topic was mothers. Two hapless mothers whose sons were wrongly accused of blowing up Mangobagh's softest targets and thrown into the Indian version of Guantanamo. She had a particular interest in this case; her husband had been the prime suspect for as little as a week, and then, as in many cases in which he had been the prime suspect or the co-accused, the truth prevailed yet again and his name was cleared. His distant cousin Qadir was still a suspect and absconding, though nobody outside of the family circle knew they were cousins.

For a sixteen-year-old, the girl spoke impressively well of motherhood. The smiling face of a strangled Rasool Hathim still poking needles into her heart every night, Noor Jahan sahiba could relate to this sense of loss the way probably even the speaker herself could not. She decided to honour the sweating girl with a glass of cold sherbet and a slice of dilkush.

Send the Jhansi Rani up.
– Noor Jahan sahiba (1951–)

Three sweating glasses of sherbet and one full orb of dilkush later, it was agreed that Noor Jahan sahiba would be honorary president of Mothers against Noose and Mehreen Malik the custodian. All the mothers and would-be mothers in the mohalla would sign a petition to the President of India, who herself was a mother. In retaliation to which, all the mothers and would-be mothers in Mehendi would sign another petition, interpreting even the slightest intention to glance through the petition from Vanity Bagh as a mark of disrespect to the 11/11 victims, and send it to the President of India, who didn't read petitions anyway.

Neither petition ever transpired. Mehreen Malik, though only for a fleeting month or so, became the talk of the mohalla, and remained the apple of hundreds of mothers' collective eye, including that of Salma Auntie's, who had famously told the NIA, though she had mistaken me for the investigator, to hang Zulfikar and bury him without letting her have a final look at him. Some even ranked Mehreen Malik as the top talent of 2010. Others wrote her off as a mere show-off.

The defence lawyer, either in a bid to project himself as a picture of confidence or to show his contempt for public campaigns and petitions, said he would be pleased to have us slapped with the death sentence. Zia's father wanted to set the lawyer's rundown office on fire but, having recently developed a sizeable respect for the law, limited his outburst to a line of expletives administered to the lawyer's junior. Then the lawyer, with an air of indifference that could have come only from too powerful a foresight, explained. A death sentence would garner support for us. We would be discussed in the national media. Human rights activists living in places we didn't even know existed would come out gagged in black clothes and carry placards showing our faces. Then we would move an appeal in the high court.

> And a word to you, Zia's father. Every word you tell my junior reaches me. Sometimes with his own additions.
>
> – Defence Lawyer (1965-)

In 2006, shortly after Benazir had been betrothed to the television dealer from Begum Bazaar, a fire raged in the kitchen of Mogul Bakery resolutely enough to bring two fire engines to the mohalla. In Ammi's memory, that was the first major fire in Vanity Bagh which had nothing to do with arson. Sharif Khan, who had waited in vain for something resembling a fire engine to arrive and had to watch fire lick his hair salon clean as a direct outcome of Pakistan's 1992 world cup victory, fumed at the sight of not one but two of them arriving, tolling their pompous bells.

> They will come and pump water into his arse when Mir can't stop farting. Chooths.
>
> – Sharif Khan (1950-)

Sparing the façade, the fire engines squeezed their way into a side road and sprayed the back of the bakery and three nearby buildings with iridescent sheets of water. The traffic on the main road had come to a standstill; inside the stalled buses there were near-stampedes for box seats to the spectacle of someone's hard-earned money going up in thick curls of smoke. At a window above the bakery signage, Benazir appeared with her recently hennaed hands and freshly plucked eyebrows, fiddling with her swanky mobile phone while her daddy's Rome was burning. She started to talk on the phone, breaking immediately into a flirtatious smile, so I deduced the Samsung super stockist was at the other end – I could even imagine his fingers dancing on the keys of a calculator as they exchanged the sound of kisses. It was a while before she spotted me amongst the crowd, looking blankly at her while everyone else had their heads cocked towards the burning chimney. She stopped talking and, holding the phone away from her face, froze at the centre of the arched window frame, staring back, her face set with the saddest smile of 2006. A diaphanous puff of smoke floated across the street, a steady hiss of water drifted up the side road; it was a moment so beautiful and painful at once that I ranked it next to the tragedy of Jack and Rose. 'Every night in my dreams, I see you ...' would have been the perfect accompaniment. To break the trance, a fireman appeared behind Benazir and asked her to evacuate the building immediately.

The crowd went home much after the fire engines did. Mir sahib put a notice on the shutters to say the shop was closed for renovation, as if no one had seen the fire engines come and go. He had a table placed in front of the shutters and heaped it with buns and bread neither fire nor firemen had thought of consuming, and stuck a second notice on the shutter which, in what I easily recognized as Benazir's hand, read: FREE FOR ALL.

As if we are living in Somalia.
– Sharif Khan (1950-)

With a serious sneer on her face, Ammi went home; I realized she had been sneering at Sharif Khan and not at Mir sahib only when she returned a few minutes later, carrying two plastic bags into which she stuffed Mir sahib's unexpected charity. Her action mobilized the crowd, and the buns and bread were gone in no time.

Somalis are a less hungry lot.
– Mrs Sharif Khan (1957-2011)

Wasim announced a fast unto death while Ammi made all kinds of burgers and sandwiches. The imam looked pleased with the big spread on the table and rubbed his palms together like hungry husbands in English movies, but when he learned the real reason for the radical departure from Ammi's usual meagre menu, he pushed the plate away and the chair back and stood up, saying eating leftovers from somebody else's kitchen gave him gas. Ammi's big eyes turned to little pools and, before they could brim over, I grabbed what I could be sued for calling a burger and took a bite from it.

'Can I have a word with you, bhai?' Wasim asked with forced civility.

'Yes,' I said. 'Tell me.'

'Not here,' he said. 'Come out.'

He led me to the door that overlooked Abbas Chacha's backyard and, leaning against the door frame with his hands crossed behind his back, asked through gritted teeth, 'Do you really want to eat leftovers from your ex-girlfriend's house, future gangster?'

How fast these kids grow up! How good they get at hitting you below the belt!

Skirting the house, I went out to the street and, strolling under the yellow light of sodium vapours, I headed to Surf XL, where I sat in a corner cubicle with a view of the main street through the tinted glass. I didn't latch the cubicle door as I did most evenings, nor did I unzip my jeans. No need for all that. I wouldn't visit the 'Frog Sex' main page today and then jump to two of my most beloved categories under the sun: 'Mature' and 'Interracial'. I went to Google Earth instead.

From the heavens, Mangobagh looked like a rambling mango orchard dotted with dwellings built for watchmen. Vanity Bagh, when zeroed in, appeared to be nothing more than a pixellated puddle, then the image cleared up and the back-to-back hoardings mounted on the roof of Imperial Hotel stood like toast glued together by blackberry jam. To the left was Franklin, looking tinier probably than it had a century ago; to the right was the light green three-storeyed block that was Mir sahib's establishment on the ground floor and residence on the upper one, topped with a water tank the size of an ice cream tub. I almost expected to find Benazir seated by the water tank, as diminutive as Barbie, as dainty and weightless as well.

Wasim knew what I was aspiring to be. He knew I had a broken heart too.

The transparent mouse had some loose components inside, and it rattled like dice every time I changed my glider's view of the city. Now I was hovering over the chequered fields beyond the Moosa River; the mausoleum where Maharaja Muneer Shah was laid to rest three years ago and his juvenile son three decades back looked like an abandoned garden. Further north were the new residential estates, down south a thin river. I was circling over the western side when a cluster of buildings enveloped in high walls caught my attention. I swooped down and down until I saw barbed wire on the walls and tall blue gates under an arched gateway. It was some kind of an institution, though the angle did not let me read what was written above the gates. There were whitewashed buildings around a large playfield and, for a moment, I wondered if it was a residential school, whether the two blocks of brick structures had been built to accommodate the boarders. There was a long line of what could be lavatories; there was something that looked like a watch tower; and three squat buildings with their own individual fences. Without caring to find out what they were, I floated away to the familiar landscape of the mohalla, looking for the alley I had left a while ago, and the little house with lots of sandwiches and burgers no one wanted to eat.

Years later, as a van with mesh wire on the windows drove me through the blue gates under an arched gateway, I had a feeling that I had been here before, but it was months before I realized where I had had a peek at this place from.

XX

The court adjourned till November 11.

~ Justice P. R. Nariman (-2012)

I had long stopped waking up on Wednesdays with an air of expectancy. I had stopped adding new entries to the list of probable reasons.

Probable reason 15: Out of sight, out of mind.

That was the last of them all. It didn't actually deserve to be on the list, for it was not a probable reason but the remotest possibility, but you need some conclusion to end a case and close the file. I would never be out of Ammi's mind no matter how long I would be out of her sight.

As Wednesdays passed without visitors, the only things that connected me to my past were the notebooks I bound. There were new covers, showing little stadiums with strategic formations or field settings, but inside were old stories, tales from Vanity Bagh. I hoped parents would attribute their wards' poor performance to the little game ideas that their notebooks came with and complain to the school, and the prison would lose orders in such huge quantities that the friendly-looking warden would have his double increment revoked, the certificate of merit snatched back and thrown away. I stopped even looking at him.

'Have you gone deaf?' he asked, knocking on my worktable with a clenched fist. 'Or have you gone mad?'

I looked up, but didn't tell him if it was my ears or my mind that had failed me. Why should I?

'I was talking to you,' he said with the hint of a smile. 'And you were talking to yourself.'

I tried to return his smile, but in my eyes he had long stopped looking friendly.

'Go,' he said, waving a hand towards the door. 'You have a visitor.'

Surprised, almost shocked, I looked around the Book Room; yes, it was Wednesday again – several inmates were missing from behind their worktables.

'But don't climb the tree and vanish like your friend did,' he said as I reached the door. 'We are already short of hands here.'

The mentioned tree, the colossal banyan, was awash in fierce close-to-noon sunlight; light streamed through its branches and stamped the mould beneath with shimmering spots. Since Zia's escape, the wardens considered the tree with a look of mild suspicion, and for the inmates it became a symbol of freedom, a ray of hope as bright as the beams that the April sun was filtering through the branches to create.

The Visitors' Room was more crowded than I remembered it from four months ago. The air was already heavy with whispers and cackling children. Having just emerged into the room of red walls I was the only one standing, except for the watchful wardens. Standing by the door I cast quick glances sideways, but there was no sign of Ammi. She would have been conspicuous in a crowd of this size: she was a large-boned woman and, as if her build was not enough to get her noticed, she borrowed Fatima's garish headdress when she came calling.

I looked from face to face, not recognizing any of them; only a lone old man with a grey beard and no moustache sitting with a long, rolled-up umbrella across his lap looked nervously at me and grudged me a smile. I recognized the umbrella before I recognized its owner. When he rose up slowly from the bench, a skullcap dangling from his fingers, I realized it was not the years of not seeing him that had made the imam look a perfect stranger; it was the absence of the skullcap on his head. Without its scalloped edge running parallel to the permanent lines of worry on his forehead, his face appeared to have grown long, his head balder than I remembered it on Eid mornings when he took off the white cap and combed his meagre hair with his long fingers before putting on a red Kabuli fez.

The imam shuffled up the aisle like a man who had had cramps a short while ago; he reached me, wheezing lightly, and sat on an empty bench with the umbrella planted firmly between his knees. It would look odd if I remained standing so I sat opposite him, pressing myself against the backrest, so our knees would not touch. Having never been inside a prison and not knowing a thing about the visiting-hour etiquette, he spied on the neighbouring set of furniture for clues, where an inmate was feeding a little girl a finger of the chocolate she had brought with her. Ammi would not have wasted time looking around, she would have started her round-up by now – on one of her visits the first thing she told me was how the imam was falling victim to a peculiar case of stage fright; he dreaded the azan, something he used to love doing so dearly and with his own sense of rhythm that Wasim and I used to blush when the muezzin's call drifted across the mohalla. He now feared his voice would be met with boos from the street. He had five three-minute ordeals to live through everyday.

Silence welled up between the benches, and a lady with dark patches under her eyes was watching us from the corner of her eye while the man fed the little girl the finger of sticky chocolate.

'How is Wasim?' I heard myself ask.

'He is completely healthy,' the imam said in a shaky voice. 'He does all the cooking now.'

'Where is Ammi?' I asked warily, a sudden chill rising up my spine. 'Why hasn't she paid me a visit the last four months?'

The imam tightened his grip around the chestnut handle of his trademark umbrella and began weeping. The lady, the little girl and her father were all looking at us now as if they had finished their family affairs and had all the time in the world to spare. The attention from across the aisle quietened the imam. Wiping his eyes, he readied himself to say something.

Junior, I have to tell you something.

– Sean Connery (1930-)

I knew what was coming. I had suspected it all along, even when I kept adding entries to my list of probabilities.

Don't get sentimental now, Dad.
Save it until we get out of here.
– Harrison Ford (1942-)

You left when you were becoming interesting.
– Sean Connery (1930-)

Rotating the handle of his umbrella, the imam recounted Ammi's final day in weepy whispers. Another eyewitness account from the mohalla where you could be miles away from the scene and still call yourself an eyewitness. The account started with the imam coming home after the night prayers to the sound of Tabu and Humera baying for water. The house was unlit, the front door half-ajar. He wandered through the house until he came upon Ammi sleeping on Wasim's bed. Only that she was not asleep, but twenty minutes away from the doors of Jannatul Firdaus. He went to the kitchen, made two glasses of tea and brought them on a tray to Wasim's bed, and tried to wake her up.

I never knew the imam had cherished such a strong filmi flourish.

His shouts brought Abbas Chacha and Noora Auntie home, and they ferried her to a clinic near the intersection where, after ten minutes of being treated on, she had a second heart attack and died.

The imam was weeping again, and the lady with the dark

patches under her eyes was looking intently at me, as if she wanted me to put my hands on the imam's knees and say something that would make him weep less. But what could I say?

> If you had been an ordinary, average father
> like the other guys' dads, you'd have understood that.
> – Harrison Ford (1942-)

The imam, as if I had demanded an explanation from him, recounted how desperately he tried to get me out on parole, just for a few hours, just till Ammi's burial was over. But the prison had banged its low iron door shut on Adv. Fakir Ansari who had sworn on Ammi's body to bring me home to carry the maiyath to the mosque, failing which at least to the kabristan to throw a fistful of dust on her grave. Riding pillion on Abbas Chacha's scooter, he swore for miles on their journey back home. Late at night, one of the suspended wardens turned up in the guise of a mourner and whisked Fatima's husband away to a patch of darkness near the alley well to mediate a deal with the imam: he would get me a four-hour parole if he was shown Zia's hideaway. The imam said he was a law-abiding citizen first, a loving father next – a statement that further strengthened my doubt about his claim of having never watched a movie in his whole life. The warden, with the diminishing confidence of a neglected hijacker, kept coming down on his demands. Any information on Zia's new phone number? Or the name of his contact person? Or his contact person's contact number? Name of the person who last saw him? Any tip-off would earn me 240 minutes of handcuffed freedom. The imam said he was helpless, the warden replied so was he.

Somewhere along the narrative, the imam had put on his skullcap, his cheeks had dried up, but his eyes still looked on the brink of watering again. I imagined him going around the little mosque after the night prayers, straightening the prayer mats with his toes, fastening windows, pausing to stare into the darkness as he latched the set of windows that overlooked the stairway, switching off the lights and finally locking up the green lattice doors. A short bicycle ride later, he would be home where Wasim cooked supper and he breakfast, where they ate in silence at a table that had mica curling at the edges.

A long ring of an electric bell ended the visiting hour. Leaning his weight on his umbrella, the imam hauled himself to his feet. Across the aisle the lady with the dark patches under her eyes looked almost accusingly at me; I appeared to have offended her by not placing my hands on the imam's knees, not mumbling comforting words to him, not giving him company when he had wept. The little girl had chocolate stains at the corners of her mouth. As the second bell rang, more sternly this time, she wrapped her hands around her father's neck and kissed him, leaving brown traces on his cheeks.

I remained at a window as the imam walked slowly along the flowerbeds, occasionally using the umbrella as his walking stick. As he started hobbling around the curving wall of the Record Room, I turned to leave. Then, as the conviction that I was never going to see him again gripped me, I retraced my steps to the window and looked out. The path was empty.

I sat still at my worktable as the Book Room slowly filled

up around me. Word had got around, and the inmates gave me sympathetic pats as they filed past me.

'I am sorry about your mother,' said the warden who, all of a sudden, started looking friendly again. 'I can report to the head warden that you are unwell. You can take a half-day off if you want.'

I said no. I told him work comforted me more than rest did. Looking hurt, he went away. Picking up a book, I opened it at random. I stared at the blank pages and waited for them to dissolve into the details of the funeral I had seen a picture of on Javed Miandad's digital camera. There was nothing to suggest that the casket suspended above a sea of white caps contained Ammi, but I was somehow sure that it was the same funeral I had been denied permission to attend. Even after several minutes had passed, even after I had turned page after page, nothing happened. The pulpy leaves remained as blank as they were meant to be.

Blank pages are white roses.
Wield your pen and fill them with fragrance.
– Shair Shoukath (1928-2010)

Vanity Bagh Poetry Club was, after all, a bad idea.
– Professor Suleiman Ilahi (1949-)

Yes, especially when Shoukath starts to recite.
– Rustom sahib (1951-)

In mid-May, the blue van with mesh wire on the windows slid silently through the blue gates to take me out of the prison for the first time in a very long time. I didn't recognize the men inside; they were not the same full-sleeved ones who had come to our house the third morning after the blast. These people wore white half-sleeved shirts and sobriety on their close-shaven faces. They spoke as little as the full-sleeved ones. But I was not sure if they were from the NIA or some other agency. A wireless, looking abandoned on a seat, kept crackling throughout the journey, airing mostly traffic news like an FM station. Then I heard the name of a hospital mentioned. One of the men picked it up, grunted a curt thank you into it and tossed it to the seat he had picked it up from, leaving two almost identical voices to swap news of minor road accidents and bottlenecks like gossips.

We must have driven about twenty minutes with no real intention of going anywhere. Then the van drove in through what looked like the back gate of a loose cluster of buildings surrounded by flint walls. In the distance were glass doors stuck with transparent hospital signs. Closer to the mesh wire windows were arrows pointing to the doctors' parking, outpatients' parking, pharmacy and canteen. Taking no heed of the arrows, the van scuttled on until the road narrowed down and was lined with cassava plantations on both sides. A lone arrow solemnly announced a mortuary was in the vicinity.

'Take a good look at the body and say just yes or no. Take your time. No hurry. But don't make any mistake,' said one of the half-sleeved men as a squat, whitewashed building appeared on the windshield. 'And don't talk to anybody else.'

When the van came to a halt outside the mortuary, they locked their fingers into mine and walked me down an empty, silent corridor to a door that looked as if it were fashioned out of a long sheet of aluminium. A short man in white clothes opened it, smiling politely at the short-sleeved men, as if all he cared about was being the perfect host in this house of the dead. It was chilly inside, and almost brilliantly lit. We were led to a row of oversized bank lockers and the man in white tugged at the handle of a locker. A long bed slid out of the wall and cold vapours wafted out.

'Take a look.'

I stood on my toes and peered in.

'Just say yes or no.'

'Yes.'

'Sure?'

I nodded in the affirmative. It was indeed Zia; except for a gash on his left temple his face was touched with little disfigurement.

'Want to take another look?'

I nodded in the negative, wondering whether he had asked if I needed another look to be doubly sure or if I would like one final look at my friend. It didn't matter how I interpreted the question; my answer would have been no either way.

The voices on the wireless now exchanged news of a religious procession that had started a while ago. One voice recommended deviation to the van. The other gave directions. I heard the places I knew make the alternate route to the prison – Begum Bazaar, Ashraf Bagh, Broadway Street, Char Bazaar intersection, Vanity Bagh.

> I wish to go and dwell in such a place
> where there is no one else.
> – Mirza Ghalib (1797–1869)

As the van swept past the intersection I slid close to the

window and rested my head against the mesh wire. A green board with a thin white border stood on the sidewalk, facing the traffic lights, reading 'Vanity Bagh'. It was a new addition, and the only thing the mohalla had got from a multi-crore town planning project to make Mangobagh more organized and, if possible, beautiful.

The traffic was sluggish, and the street rolled slowly away from the mesh wire window.

Jerome Pinto was leaning against a motorcycle parked outside Akbar Electricals, talking on his phone, most probably to Clara D'Costa, and smoking at the same time. Haja Stores stood empty and was being repainted; it must have changed hands once again. The man who was leaning over the vegetable cart in front of the Bata store was either Abbas Chacha or his younger brother Taufeeq – both had the same kind of backside. Under Franklin stood Mary Pinto, seriously irritated with something; I was almost sure it was her brother who had caused her discomfort as usual. The green lattice door of the mosque was wide open, framing a few silhouettes kneeling down in prayer. Mir sahib was counting money behind his counter. A beggar stood outside the shop, waiting for his benevolence. Above him, Benazir's window stood closed.

Beside the Irani Café, in the alley of Abu Hathim sahib's bungalow, a group of small boys was playing football with the same disrespect for soccer rules with which we had once treated the game.

Then the cobbled path that led to my home came into view. Wasim was walking down the alley with Fatima's second son. They were almost out on the sidewalk when the van passed the mouth of the alley.

'Wasim,' I screamed. 'Wasim.'

He didn't hear me. He grabbed the boy's wrist as they stepped onto the pavement.

'Bilawal,' I yelled louder. The boy looked suspiciously around. For a moment his gaze fell on the mesh wire window, but at the next it drifted away. Lifting his head, he said something to Wasim. They laughed together and then walked sprightly away.

The moment the rickshaw stopped, your abba said,
'This is Vanity Bagh, where we will build our home
and make it heaven-like.'
– Bushra Jabbari (1962-2012)

Acknowledgements

Saugata Mukherjee, Publisher.
Pallavi Narayan, Editor.
M. G. Parameswaran, Big Boss.
Joe Thaliath, Big Brother.
Kanishka Gupta, Agent.
Abdulla Khan, Friend.
Omar, Son.
Shameena, Wife.